RISE TO THE SUN

LEAH JOHNSON

Scholastic Press / New York

Library of Congress Cataloging-in-Publication Data available

ISBN 978-1-338-66223-8

1 2021

Printed in the U.S.A.   23
First edition, July 2021

Book design by Stephanie Yang

TO THE BLACK GIRLS WHO HAVE BEEN
TOLD THEY'RE TOO MUCH AND TO THE ONES
WHO DON'T BELIEVE THEY'RE ENOUGH:
YOU ARE THE WORLD'S MOST BEAUTIFUL SONG.

Rise to the Sun is a novel that celebrates the communal joy of live music spaces and the ferocious vibrance of first love. To get full enjoyment from what I hope will be an uplifting reading experience, some readers may prefer to know ahead of time that this book does include references to parental loss, panic attacks, gun violence, and nonconsensual image sharing.

Love,

Leah

FARMLAND
MUSIC AND ARTS FESTIVAL
FRIDAY

"This is our kingdom.
Out here, nobody can tell us
we're not the greatest."

–Pop Top (née Jackie Anderson)
at the Coachella Valley Music
and Arts Festival, April 2018

OLIVIA

FRIDAY MORNING

My best friend has always been the first person I run to when it's time to blow up my life.

The radio is cranked up as loud as it can go in Imani's SUV, and both of our heads are tilted back, shouting lyrics at the roof of the car. This feeling isn't the explosion I came to her begging for at the beginning of summer three months ago—when I was sad and frustrated and heartbroken *again*—but it feels right. It feels the way things only feel when you're with your best friend in the world, on your way to your first music festival, with the rubble of a disastrous junior year behind you.

Feels like possibility.

"I'm not saying love isn't real! I'm just saying, statistically, there's no way every time you claim to have been in love it actually *was love*," she shouts during the drum solo of the song currently blasting over the speakers.

She opens her mouth for a Twizzler and leans toward me without taking her eyes off the road as she creeps forward in the line of cars. She's wearing one of her many pairs of designer sunglasses, her only real fashion indulgence, but I can see her carefully threaded eyebrows raise expectantly behind them. I do my due diligence as an A1 passenger and feed it to her.

She chews and swallows before waving a hand around to emphasize her point.

"I read a study about it. On average, you'd have to have at least two long-term relationships, one long-distance relationship, four one-night stands, and one live-in relationship before falling in love even once. You haven't run the necessary trials yet. The odds of any of your relationships having been real love are pretty low, given the data."

Imani Garrett and her odds. Imani and her *data*. Sometimes her brain works too hard for her to see what I see—that there's no way you can math your way into finding love. Like every great love song has ever taught me, it takes trial and error. And if you're me, it takes more trials than I can count and more errors than should be humanly possible.

It's hot outside, I can tell by the way the volunteers who wave us forward are sweating through their bright orange FARMLAND

4

VOLUNTEER T-shirts, but inside the car it's perfect. The air conditioner is humming and the bass is pounding and we're thrumming with anticipation—the best kind of nerves. The kind of nerves that promise a weekend big enough to change something, change *everything*. And despite the fact that Imani is trying to use her pesky logic to convince me that my heart isn't actually working overtime, this is exactly what I need right now.

The frontwoman of the band, Teela Conrad, starts belting, and for the moment, all talk of my catastrophic romantic history and my most recent failed relationship is forgotten.

I live for moments like these. As Imani shouts along to the lyrics and beats her hands against the steering wheel in time with the music, I can almost convince myself that she's as out of control as I am. That somewhere deep down in that brilliant, refined brain, is the same type of restlessness just screaming to get out that exists in mine. Those moments are always fleeting though. Because she will always turn off the radio and become herself once more.

I'm still looking for my off switch.

"Hey, Farmers!" One of the volunteers says as we pull into the check-in station. She smiles brightly at me and I beam my widest smile. I can already tell that these are my people. "You girls look ready for a good time!"

"Yeah, some of us more than others." Imani presses pause on the screen in her dash that's currently controlling the Spotify playlist, and just like that, she's cranky again. As if I could forget that the Farmland Music and Arts Festival is most certainly not her idea of a good time.

She puts the car in park so we can hop out as the volunteers scour the car for the festival's no-no's: no pets, no weapons, no drugs. As we wait, my loose-fitting mini dress immediately starts sticking to my skin thanks to the humidity of northern Georgia in August, but I keep smiling anyway. Nothing can bring me down today, not even a reluctant best friend and a lifetime of ruined romances and a phone buzzing with text messages from a mom who thinks I'm currently at a weekend youth retreat with Imani's nonexistent church.

I can't even bring myself to feel guilty about the ridiculous, borderline-blasphemous lie I had to tell her to get here.

I'm not religious in the way my mom is, obviously. Her church is in a sanctuary with pews and ministers and a collection plate that goes around for the offering. My church is the press of bodies together in a crowd, the pulse of a bass guitar vibrating under our feet, and a lead singer preaching the gospel of rebellion and revolution and love through beautiful harmonies and perfect chord progressions. Some people find salvation in a stained-glass building, other people find it in a basement punk show.

"This is a bad idea, Liv," Imani says, leaning forward like she's going to put her elbows on the hood of the car, but deciding against it when she remembers how hot the surface of it must be. It's almost like she's reading my mind. "There are so many other things you should be worrying about this weekend. Like, I don't

6

know, the judicial hearing, perhaps?" Her voice takes on that exasperated and still somehow fond tone it always takes when she's slipping into mother-hen mode. "It's taking you forever to decide what to say—you can't just wing something like this."

I can't see her eyes behind her tinted lenses, but I know she's narrowing them. I don't want to talk about the hearing. I don't want to so much as think about it. And I refuse to.

"We're not talking about that." My voice comes out quicker and with more edge than I intend for it to. I immediately try to lighten the mood. "We should be talking about the fact that my best friend is a literal genius who is practically being handed early decision to U Chicago on a silver platter!"

I might want the attention off me, but I mean it. Imani spent all summer doing research with a doctor at the University of Chicago, and she's got a pretty solid in there next fall. She's brilliant, and beautiful—brown-skinned and self-assured. She's got it all together. Too bad her big brain hasn't figured out how to fix mine.

Imani blushes, embarrassed suddenly by my compliment, and says, "Whatever. Don't try to change the subject. You have to—"

And because the Farmland volunteers are my people, my comrades, my buddies in arms, Imani doesn't get to finish that statement before we're getting the all-clear and being directed toward where our campsite is going to be. As much as I love Imani and value her opinion, I'm almost always grateful when her train of thought gets derailed.

Imani hadn't wanted to come to this festival at all. And like so many other times before, had to be persuaded by the very real, extremely dire stakes of my most recent heartbreak. It was still fall, but already my junior year had been a series of relationship-related catastrophes, the last of which rendered me both a social outcast at school and a complete shame to my mom's parentage at home.

In the immediate fallout, I'd done what any logical girl would do: I called my best friend and asked her to pick me up so we could hit the McDonald's drive thru and I could cry into an Oreo McFlurry in the parking lot as God intended. "Imani, please please *please* let's do something this summer. Something good. Something far away from here," I had begged through tears. I was already thinking months into the future. I needed something to get me through the rest of the school year, otherwise I might not survive it with my sanity intact.

"Olivia, okay, come on." Her voice took on her soothing post-breakup tone. The kind of tone people use on scared woodland creatures and, apparently, sixteen-year-old girls whose hearts have been ripped out and run over by their ex-boyfriend's stupid Dodge Charger. "You're so much better off without this one-ply toilet paper equivalent of a human being in your life."

"But, I"—hiccup—"wanted him"—hiccup—"to be"—blows nose into fancy aloe-infused tissues—"the oneeeeeeeeeee!"

"I know," she said, her eyes never leaving mine. I wiped my nose on my sleeve and she reached for her family-size hand sanitizer.

She held it out at me until I opened my palm. She squirted some and then continued. "I know you did."

I am very good at getting my heart broken. Some might even call me an impeccable *heartbreakee*. But my real secret talent seems to be getting my heart broken while en route to ruining someone's life. Loving me—or more often than not, having *me* love *you*—is a surefire blueprint for disaster.

Imagine me as the Fab Five from *Queer Eye*'s unknowingly evil twin. Instead of sweeping into your life and fixing your split ends, making your condo *Architectural Digest* ready, and revamping your wardrobe, I say the wrong things and do the wrong things and have been the mayor of the city of Too Much, Too Soon since the day I was born.

But not Imani. By some stroke of luck, I got the kind of best friend whose magical power is finding solutions when mine seems to be creating problems. She's one of the few people in the universe I have yet to chase off. There are a lot of reasons to love her, obviously, but the fact that she stays by my side is right there at the top of the list. Next to her impeccable taste in music.

I hate that it always ends up like this, that *I* always end up like this. But at least I have Imani to help pull me out of every grave I dig for myself.

"Let's just go somewhere! Anywhere, it doesn't matter." I could feel that telltale prickle of urgency at the base of my neck that I get sometimes when I need to do something major: cut my hair, jump headfirst into a new relationship, try to sign up for the Peace Corps at fourteen by "borrowing" my older sister's ID and claiming it as my own. "What about a road trip? We could see, like, monuments and stuff."

Imani snorted. "You hate monuments."

I leaned my forehead against the dash and groaned. Part of the problem here has always been the fact that Imani is the one with the car, so she is ultimately the decider of all heartbreak-healing excursions. This was yet another occasion where the lack of four-wheeled mobility really limited my options.

"Yeah, okay, so I think they're mostly boring and a poor use of taxpayer dollars." I blew my nose into the tissue. "So, we go see something else, then."

"I think you're forgetting a few crucial details. One: Your mom will never let you go. Two: You're broke."

"Counterpoint: My mom hates me anyway so another notch on that belt won't hurt much. And I have a few hundred saved up from the car fund, remember?" It's not like I wasn't working on the car thing. It was just taking a while. Like my entire high school career, a while.

The radio was turned way down, but even through my tears, I could identify the low hum of Imani's favorite band playing in the background. Kittredge was pretty much a constant staple when riding in her car. Her favorite band in part because of their music, but mostly for Davey Mack, their scraggly redheaded bassist and

Teela Conrad's more eccentric co-lead singer—the only person on the planet Imani had ever admitted any type of attraction to.

Imani opened her mouth to respond but stopped immediately when she caught the melody that was playing from the speakers. She reached for the volume and turned it up to full blast. "I'm just a girl who rose to the bait, and you're still the boy who tempted my fate!"

She belted the entire verse before relaxing back into her seat with a sigh and turning the volume back down.

"Ugh, I can't believe I'm missing their entire tour this summer."

This conversation was familiar too. Imani had missed Kittredge on their last two summer tours because of the early college program she did at the University of Chicago, and the tour before that because she said the tickets she bought ended up being fakes. Which was perfect for me because I ended up needing her to hold my hand through a heartbreak that night anyway.

And now, as soon as they finished the European leg of their tour, they were rumored to be going on hiatus.

In that moment, I thought back to poring over their tour schedule with her when it was announced months before, and like a cartoon light bulb practically appearing over my head, I suddenly knew what to do. The last date on their tour was headlining a massive music festival in Georgia at the end of August. It was a few days after Imani got back from Chicago, and a week before our senior year started. I could get my road trip, Imani could get to see the love of her life, and for one brief weekend before going back to school and the hellscape of what that would mean for me, we could have the time of our lives.

"Music festivals are dangerous," she hedged. "Heat stroke? Dehydration? A deranged gunman shooting up the place? Don't look at me like that. Don't you remember what happened at that festival in Las Vegas?"

"I think you worry too much," I said. Imani's always been a stickler about anything that involves even the slightest chance of danger. I blame the fact that she's been listening to BBC World Service on NPR with her dad since before she knew how to talk. Too much news makes a person paranoid.

"Well one of us has to."

It hadn't been an easy sell, not even with the convincing pitch. She pushed back with statistic after statistic about everything that could go wrong, but if I know how to do anything, it's figure out ways to make people cave. And her love of Davey Mack will always win out over her better logic. I can't say I'm not grateful for having found her one weak point.

Before she agreed, she had one stipulation.

"You can't do what you always do," she said, hesitating over the order button when we were buying our tickets on our phones. The dull yellow-ish light from the McDonald's sign streamed through the window and illuminated the inside of the car. "When we get there, you have to promise me you won't decide to spend the weekend hooking up with someone new."

She looked at me with the type of openness Imani only ever

allows herself when the two of us are together, and I knew what came next was going to be important. "This has to be a me-and-you thing, okay? A best friend weekend." She held out her pinky and I linked mine through it. We kissed our thumbs to seal the promise, the same way we'd done since we became best friends. She bought her ticket, and immediately began searching the rest of the Farmland website. "And I want to ride the Ferris wheel while we're there. According to the website they have one. So we can't miss it."

She ducked her head as she said it, like she was embarrassed to have such a mundane thing on her bucket list, like the only thing she was allowed to hope for was a Nobel Prize and a Fields Medal or whatever.

I thought back to all the times Imani had shown up somewhere just because I asked, and how much I loved her for that. After everything Imani had done for me, keeping this promise would be the least I could do. One epic weekend where the two of us could see our favorite bands, get heinous tan lines, and have an experience so fun it would sustain me through the miserable senior year I have ahead of me.

"Deal." I nodded.

Because that's what best friends do.

TONI

FRIDAY MORNING

My summer is ending the way every summer of my life that I can remember has ended: setting up camp in the relentless sun of Farmland Music and Arts Festival's seven-hundred-acre land next to a person that gets it, gets me. It's perfect. It's familiar. Until the person across from me speaks up, and I remember with startling clarity that nothing is the same as it has been in summers prior.

"Toniiiiiii," Peter whines from his seat in the grass. "This would go so much faster if you would just let me help."

Peter pulls off his worn Oakland A's hat to shake out his black curls before readjusting it, brim to the back. He's got his legs crossed just a few feet away from where I'm setting up camp, and I'm doing my best to ignore the big, brown, imploring puppy-dog eyes he keeps shooting my way. They're almost irresistible, even for me.

I grunt instead of responding and pull the netting more securely over the top of the tent. Things are much quicker when I just do them myself. It's no offense to him, it's just a fact.

"Being an island isn't in our nature as humans, T-Bone! Just look at John Tyler. They called him the 'president without a party'—never even stood a chance at a second term. You know why? He isolated himself." He's clearly been streaming one of those documentaries they used to show us in APUSH for fun again. When the only response I offer is a stare that says *You're earnestly comparing me to a dead white man in conversation again, Peter?* he sputters, "Okay so maybe the aesthetics are a little different but the point stands!"

I wince at his volume and he adds, "Oops. Sorry, T. I get riled up about the pre-Reagan presidents." He taps on his phone screen and brightens. "Hey! Someone just posted that they saw Bonnie Harrison at the taco cart. We have to go. Right? Definitely. I know how you feel about Sonny Blue."

He's right, Sonny Blue is my favorite queer-fronted folk-soul duo of all time, but I'm too focused on the task at hand to answer. He waits a beat before speaking again. Peter has done this since the day we met at this festival six years ago. He has no problem filling in all the spaces in a conversation that should, theoretically, be occupied by me. I try not to say more than absolutely necessary though. This, like my working best alone, is yet another brick to add to the impenetrable Toni Foster Fortress.

Peter is the only one who's ever managed to work his way past my defenses. Six years ago, our campsites were right next to each other out here—him with his Uncle Rudy and me with my dad—and I couldn't shake him the entire weekend. No matter how withdrawn or sullen I became, Peter just kept popping up, asking questions, insisting that I try his signature s'mores recipe over our shared bonfire. It was like he didn't even notice how unsociable I was. I couldn't seem to shake him. And eventually, somewhere between his forty-third fun fact about a dead president and his twelfth story about breaking a limb due to his ungainly awkwardness, I forgot that I wanted to.

He stands up and it's like watching a clown unfolding as they climb out of those tiny cars—how did he ever manage to look so small? He throws his arms around my shoulders, even though it's pushing 95 degrees under the midday sun and I'm in the middle of stomping a stake into the ground, so he just narrowly misses getting kneed in his ribs. He squeezes me hard like he's afraid I'm going to try and escape, which goes to show how well he knows me.

"I love you anyway, my platonic life partner," he whispers. And for a second, I'm tempted to return the line, out of instinct alone. *When people say they love you, you tell them you love them back*, my brain reminds me. But I don't really do that sort of thing.

I pat his arm twice, suddenly and overwhelmingly eager to get out of this embrace and onto what we came here for. This isn't a weekend for declarations of our BFF status, or time for Peter to employ his mom's "lead with love" child-rearing techniques to therapize me. We're not even here for the shows, though that's a nice added bonus. We're here so I can figure my life out. That's it.

I can breathe a little easier when Peter pulls away, and I almost feel guilty about it. But I don't let myself. If I make room for anything other than drive, I think I might just lose it. I take a deep breath and finish stomping the stake into the ground instead. And just like that, the campsite resembles the way it looked last year and the year before that and every year since I was old enough to walk.

When I feel myself drifting toward what—who—it's missing though, I shake my head as if I can physically clear it. I try to focus on the world moving around me. The crack of our neighbors opening two cans of Pabst Blue Ribbon, a feather-light laugh from a campsite across the way, the sound of the Farmland radio station playing through the speakers of my truck.

"And don't forget to sign up for the Golden Apple competition!" The emcee's voice is so boisterous and radio-artificial, it's easy to cling to. "It's a time-honored Farmland tradition, and we have reason to believe that this year is going to be extra special. Right, Carmen?"

A woman's voice chimes in, raspy yet commercial. "Definitely, Jason. This year's judges are the best lineup we've had in years.

A life-changing opportunity for these competitors for sure. And we can't forget the other exciting competition this weekend: #FoundAtFarmland . . ."

My attention begins to drift as the hosts keep talking. Farmland is famous for a lot of things—being one of the biggest music festivals in the country, essentially launching the careers of some of the biggest bands in the world—but the thing they hold in the highest esteem is the Golden Apple. A talent competition that gives amateur musicians a chance to play in front of a panel of headliners as judges, and whoever wins gets a chance to play on stage with one of the bands on the last day of the festival.

It's one of the biggest draws the festival has to offer, and it's a massive hit every year. This year, it's being held for the chance to perform with Kittredge, one of the biggest alt-rock bands in the world and coincidentally, my dad's former employers. He tour managed for them for most of my life, and before them a slew of other bands out of the Midwest, but never any that took off the way Kittredge did.

"You hear that, Toni?" Peter calls from inside the truck, where he's attempting to charge his phone in my finicky lighter outlet. "They're talking about your big break!"

He leans his entire upper body out the window and air guitars with no rhythm. I want to laugh, but the idea of a big break—of a moment on a stage that determines your entire life—is too close for comfort. I don't want to be famous. I don't want to be a star. I just want some answers.

I pull the hard case that now houses my favorite acoustic guitar—a beautiful mahogany Fender my parents gave me for my fifteenth birthday—out of the truck bed and lean it against the side of the truck. It's adorned with stickers from all over the world, designations of all the places it's gone. The limited untouched spots are reminders of where it has yet to go. Incredible big cities, dusty dive bars, and huge venues all decorate its exterior. It's a tapestry, cohesive in its narrative: a patchwork life that took my dad farther away from me than I could ever wrap my head around.

But right in the center, shiny and fresh where the rest have dulled with time and wear, is the newest addition to the bunch. A crimson and cream WELCOME HOME, HOOSIER sticker from my freshman orientation at Indiana University last month. Mom must have snuck it on there when I wasn't paying attention as I was packing last night. I'm almost surprised she didn't slap her Maurer School of Law sticker on there too just so I don't forget exactly where I'm supposed to be headed. The sight of it makes my stomach churn, just like every other reminder of where I'm supposed to be headed next week.

I know Peter doesn't quite understand why this is so important to me or why I end the conversation every time he tries to talk to me about college, though I know he'd do his best if I tried to explain it. It's just that Peter is all about big dreams and big loves. His dad is this huge mixed-media artist who sells his installations for like a billion dollars per piece, and his mom runs an Etsy shop hawking artisanal jewelry to other white women that's designed to help them find their "soul source"—whatever that means.

Peter could tell them he wanted to major in Bowling Industry Technology and they'd be happy (he did briefly entertain this for a month in tenth grade after watching a documentary on the history of the bowling ball). The Menons are the kind of family that choose passion over logic every time. And it's worked out for them. But it's not like that for most of us.

I busy myself with arranging our air mattress inside the tent while Peter drums up conversation with our neighbors, a couple of girls in sorority tank tops and high ponytails with a UT Knoxville bumper sticker on their Jeep. As grateful as I am that he agreed to come with me this weekend, I breathe a little easier at the moment alone. I can feel myself slipping, despite my best efforts to swallow down all the anxiety that's been bubbling up in me since the moment we got to Farmland. All the memories that refuse to stay locked away, all the promises my dad made to me that are now going to go unfulfilled.

The thing is, no one could have prepared for the way we lost my dad. But that didn't change the gnawing emptiness that had taken up residence inside me over the past eight months.

I don't know if I believe in a higher power or life after death or any of the stuff the minister said at my dad's funeral. But countless summers spent at the greatest music festival in the world, on a former farm in Rattle Tail, Georgia, along with sixty thousand other music fans, watching sets from on top of his sunburnt shoulders taught me one inalienable truth: that somewhere in the light-years of space between the spiritual and the scientific, between the known and the ineffable, there's live music.

There's Jimi Hendrix playing a two-hour set at Woodstock that revolutionizes rock and roll forever. There's Beyoncé becoming the first Black woman to ever headline Coachella and delivering a performance that redefines a culture. There's Bob Dylan going electric at Newport Folk in '65 and Queen reuniting at Live Aid twenty years later. Live music is a True Thing: It holds the keys to the universe, and all you have to do is pay attention.

If you ever have a question, my dad taught me that live music held the key. And I can't help but believe that too. Because I've never been more in need of guidance than right now.

My mom has made it clear since I was a kid that what she wants for me is stability, consistency. That she wants something more for me than the type of life my dad led. I have to do something concrete, something *real*. Which means college. Not because she'd punish me or cut me off or kick me out or any of that if I didn't go, but because it would break her heart to see me end up like my dad. Constantly running toward a dream that would never be realized.

I won't do that to her. I can't.

I want to trust my mom's belief that starting at IU will give me the direction I've been searching for, but my gut is screaming at me that my purpose isn't to sit in a classroom in Bloomington reading the Brontë sisters and trying to recover from a Kappa party the night before. When I think about college, my hands start to shake and I can barely breathe. But when I think about not going, I draw a complete blank.

My mom has no doubts that the reason why I've been flailing so spectacularly in the past few months was a result of my grief. But the bigger part, the even scarier part, is that I'm almost eighteen—almost a bona fide adult—and I have no idea what I want to do with my life. And I know now, with stark clarity, that none of us has time to waste when it comes to figuring it out. My dad was a prime example of that.

My dad always said when people get on stage they just *know*. It's what happened to him. When he was eighteen, he picked up his guitar, and he played in front of an audience for the first time during an open mic at a coffeeshop in Bloomington. And just like that, he was sure that being a part of putting good music out into the world was how he wanted to spend the rest of his life. Even if I wasn't going to be in the music industry like him, he said, there was no lying on a stage.

Whatever you were running from, whatever you should be running toward, would reveal itself under all those lights.

This festival isn't where he found his purpose, but it could be where I find mine. It has to be.

It's too much to explain to Peter, to anyone, so I don't.

"Toni!" As usual, I hear Peter before I see him.

I run a hand over my face and duck back out of the tent to meet him. When I look at him, he's patting his stomach where his cropped Fleetwood Mac T-shirt leaves his skinny tanned torso exposed. He's gotten really into bringing back crop tops for guys lately. According to him, *The Fresh Prince did it! Fragile masculinity shouldn't keep us from embracing the best of nineties fashion.*

I can hear his stomach growl even from a few feet away. He wiggles his eyebrows at me. "Taco stand?"

I nod. I grab my phone, even though the signal is awful out here, and start in the direction of the Core—the center of the festival where everything from food to merch to the stages reside. We make it about five minutes before a flurry of movement out of the corner of my eye stops me. My first reaction is the quick uptick of fear at the sight of anything moving this fast and unpredictably, until I realize what I'm looking at.

There's a girl tangled up in the lime green nylon of her tent. She's wearing a hot pink dress that would probably be better suited for some artsy date night at the Indianapolis Museum of Art than a music festival, jumbo box braids up in a bun that's so big I'm surprised it doesn't throw off her entire center of gravity, and a huge pair of heart-shaped sunglasses that are clearly more form than function.

I've seen a lot of stuff at Farmland in my day, but rarely someone so woefully ill-equipped to set up camp.

"Actually," I start, my voice rough from disuse, "Go on without me. I'm gonna . . ."

I jerk my head in the direction of the girl tangled up in the tent.

Peter smiles. "That's the Farmland spirit! Say no more, friendo. I'll grab you the best gluten-free option at the taco cart."

"Wait! Can you sign me up for the Golden Apple while you're there?" I tell him to put my first and middle name down instead of my first and last, just in case. I don't want any chance of nepotism getting in the way of things.

We should have gotten in last night so that I could sign up earlier—they only have room for about fifty acts per day—but Peter was too tired to drive after his flight to Indianapolis to meet me, and we planned on taking off early this morning anyway. It didn't help that we ended up getting a flat around Nashville and Peter practically broke a finger just jumping out of the car to try and help me change it.

He salutes as he practically skips away. While he leaves, I take a few steps toward the girl, who's now so wrapped up in her tent that she looks a little bit like a mummy.

"Hey," I call out. When she doesn't respond, I realize it's because my volume is too low. Sometimes I forget how to calibrate it when talking to anyone that's not Peter or my mom—like my voice gets caught in my throat. "Hey!"

The girl's eyes lock with mine for half a second, like she can't figure out whether or not I'm talking to her. And she immediately faceplants into the grass.

OLIVIA

FRIDAY AFTERNOON

I don't mean to stare, however I am but a mere mortal with a limited attention span and an eye for beauty.

It doesn't hurt that the beauty in question is a girl who is so deeply out of my league, we're talking Jules Verne status. And I'm not going there again. No, Olivia Brooks is no longer doing the chasing. She's no longer doing the catching. She's no longer diving heart-first into crushes that will inevitably lead to ruin. I'm so past that.

But there's no harm in just watching the girl walking down the dirt car lane from ours as she pretends not to smile at something her friend is saying. It's totally inconsequential to me when she takes off her wide-brimmed cowboy hat and shakes her locs loose like she's in some sort of conditioner commercial. I'm definitely not moved by the fact that her legs look impossibly long in her cutoff shorts and they're a shade of brown so rich that sort of reminds me of Chiron from the *Moonlight* poster—and they're so shiny, my God, how can one person's legs look like that? What is her skincare routine?

But then she's walking in my direction, and I'm so very much not cut out for this camping thing no matter how many Farmland message boards I read before coming here, and I'm tangled in the stupid mesh netting of the tent I bought online three weeks ago, and she's shouting at me and—

I'm on the ground, an Olivia-sized heap surrounded by lime green nylon and aluminum tent poles. I can just sense that my bun has been knocked askew and my new sunglasses are cocked to the side. There's precious little that could be more embarrassing than this. And I've been in my fair share of embarrassing situations in front of cute people. Just ask River Brody about the punchbowl incident at the freshman farewell dance.

If Imani weren't off in the Core trying to get a better cell signal to call her parents and check in, I'm sure she'd be standing off to the side, making that pursed-lip Olivia-how-do-you-always-end-up-like-this expression before moving to help me up. But as it stands, the person looming over me is all stone face and shiny Wayfarer sunglasses that reflect me back to myself.

"Huh." Great Skin blocks the sun as she leans over me. Up close, I can see every detail of her face, from her septum piercing to the way one of her eyebrows is just a little less arched than the other. She rubs the back of her neck and pushes her sunglasses down slightly to meet my eyes. I might say something about it, might make a regrettably flirtatious comment perfectly tailored to the type of person I think she might be, just from a quick glance, but the tent is tight around me, pinning my arms to my body, and falling down sort of kicked my adrenaline into high gear and Great Skin is just *staring* and nothing about that is good for my lungs.

They do their best, the wheezy little guys, but just about anything can send them into overdrive. And—yup. There it is.

I wiggle around, gasping, trying to get my arms free so I can reach the inhaler currently nestled in my fanny pack.

"Are you okay?" Great Skin says, and I'd almost be impressed at how nonplussed she seems by the whole me having an asthma attack at her feet thing if I weren't, you know, struggling to get air into my lungs.

"My. *Inhaler*," I barely manage to get out. I jerk my head in the direction of the fanny pack, willing her to pull her shit together for the sake of my literal life, and then she can go right back to being beautiful and goddess-like.

"Your wha—Oh my God."

Her expression shifts to one of complete fear as she drops to the ground and fumbles through the fanny pack until she comes up with my hot pink inhaler and shoves it into my mouth. I don't even think about it when she presses down and releases the albuterol. I breathe in deeply like I've done since I was a kid and my mom used to have to handle my meds. I hold it in for the requisite ten seconds, and like she knows what she's doing, she presses it again.

When I feel my heart rate begin to settle, and air start to come a little easier, I let my head flop back into the grass with a sigh. Great Skin does the same. She lays down right next to my sushi rolled form and heaves out a relieved breath of her own.

It's maybe thirty seconds before I say, "Hey, um, sorry for the life-or-death moment there before, but would you mind giving me a hand?"

It's like my voice jolts her out of her own head, and she instantly sits up. She pushes my body a little to the left, hand gentle but insistent, while pulling the netting with the other. Before I know it, I'm back on my feet and eternally indebted to a stranger with a somehow perfectly stoic face. Despite everything, she manages to stand up, brush herself off, and look no worse for wear.

I want to reach up and squish her cheeks together, just to ease her expression. She was easier to read before, when she was afraid for me, but now she looks sort of like a statue. Beautiful, but emotionless. Years of training, of standing in front of beautiful, unavailable people and seeing both a challenge and a home, have taught me that if I bat my eyes a certain way, or laugh at a joke that wasn't all that funny, I could eventually get a reaction from her. One that would make me the center of her universe for as long as I had her attention.

And it would feel good at the start—being noticed, shedding my skin to become someone worth keeping her eyes locked on for the length of our interaction. But it wouldn't end feeling good. And Imani is right. I have to stop thinking that way. I have to stop inviting the devil to my doorstep and wondering why I keep getting burned.

"You okay?" she asks, and I realize I've been staring for a beat too long. She waves her hand at the rubble of the campsite behind me and straightens her Ray-Bans. "I could, um, help."

"Oh my God, yes! Please." It's already an inhumane temperature since me and Imani arrived so close to noon. We had a gas station burrito incident that incapacitated Imani about three hours after we'd left Indy this morning. I'm still trying to put the whole thing out of my mind. We both had our pride bruised in the bathroom of that Speedway, to be honest.

I step out of my tent cocoon so that she can help herself to the materials, and immediately remember why the message boards also said to be careful about going barefoot around a campsite. A sharp pain shoots through my foot, and I realize I've stepped on one of those stupid pointy metal hook things that are supposed to keep the tent in the ground.

I wince, and Great Skin immediately reaches for my arm.

"Come on." She looks down at my foot. "I have first aid."

I don't even argue as she almost completely supports my weight and walks me to Imani's SUV. She helps me hop up onto the hatch, and promises to be right back. I straighten myself out while she rushes down the car lane to get her first aid kit from her truck. I wish I had a mirror, but since I don't, I make do with a simple inventory of my current state. I smooth down my mini dress, adjust my bun, and clean my sunglasses off before she comes back with a small plastic red box with the white medical plus symbol on top.

I drop my hands into my lap like I wasn't just trying to get photo-ready moments before, a little embarrassed even though I probably shouldn't be. She looks like the kind of person who just rolls out of bed flawless, makeup-free yet perfect complexion, and I envy that ease.

"Very official," I say, since she's gone silent again. "I can't believe I forgot to bring a first aid kit. It's like the first thing every message board said to bring."

She hums but doesn't respond, squirts some hand sanitizer into her palms, rubs it in, and then reaches for my foot. She sets to work with Neosporin and an assured touch, and her silence makes me jittery. I *really* don't do well with awkward silences.

"Normally it takes until a second date before people unveil the foot fetish."

If I could facepalm hard enough to project myself back in time to before I said that, I totally would.

"I'm more of a hand girl myself," she says, deadpan. "But thanks."

At that, I laugh so loud it's probably a little rude, if her confused expression is anything to go from. I realize that she's saved my life, offered to set up my campsite, and repaired my foot after a feat of my particular brand of clumsiness, and I don't even know her name. She smooths the bandage over my heel and eases my foot back down before I extend my hand.

"I'm Olivia." She takes it after a little too long and shakes once. "I promise I'm normally more together than this. And that my jokes usually land with a splash and not a thud."

"You don't say." Her voice is barely audible, but I can see the way one side of her mouth quirks up clear as day. "Toni." She puts her first aid kit into her fanny pack and shrugs. "When you've been here as many times as I have, you don't forget your Band-Aids."

Instead of continuing the conversation, Toni gets right to business. She collects all the stray tent debris that I've left scattered around the campsite and doesn't even pull out any directions before taking the pieces and making right everything I pretty much destroyed. Her phone vibrates next to me where she set it on the hatch along with the first aid kit.

"Toni?" I pick it up and hold it out to her. "Someone's calling you."

When she reaches for it, she immediately turns it on speaker and sets it in one of the camping chairs so that her hands remain free to work.

"Bad news, T-Bird!" A guy's voice crackles over the speaker, and Toni immediately stops what she's doing. She goes still all over. The guy continues like he doesn't even expect a response. "All the solo slots for the Golden Apple are filled."

She picks up her phone slowly, clicks it off speaker, and brings it to her ear so all I can hear is her end of the conversation.

"That's not possible," she whisper-shouts. She shakes her head as he responds. She adds quieter, almost inaudible, "Peter, they can't be. I'm not—I can't be a duo."

The Golden Apple. It's all over every message board about this festival. If I thought for even a second that my experience in the back row of intermediate chorus would be enough to get me anywhere, I would've entered myself just for the principle of the thing. But the way Toni's face looks right now, completely lost, I know this wasn't just a thing she wanted to do for her scrapbook.

And just like that, a different type of plan begins to come together. No wardrobe changes, no shifting my personality to be something I think she might like me to be—a plan that can help pull things together instead of my usual brand of destruction. She needs someone to compete with. I need a distraction.

She hangs up and drops down into the chair beside her. I hop off the hatch and tap her on her shoulder. She just barely turns around, and when she does, it's almost like she'd forgotten I was there.

I've become kind of a master at assuming the roles people want me to play. I know everything you could possible need to know about free-range chicken farming from dating Hilton from Future Famers of America. I got incredibly good at drawing compelling signs when I was with Brandon, the president of Park Meade High School's PETA chapter. I even considered signing up for Peace Corps when Jenna from AP Lit said she'd only ever be with a girl who was dedicated to public service.

I'm a chameleon, constantly shifting to match whatever's around me.

But the thing about changing your skin to become something or someone else is it requires constant maintenance to keep up. And when I can't—when the cracks in the surface start to show— that's when I become a person who does more harm than good.

My hands sweat at the thought of what it looks like when I get involved in someone's life, when I hurt them without meaning to. I wipe them on the hem of my dress and shake my head to clear it. No, this weekend I'm letting go of all of that. I've only packed my favorite dresses, my cutest sandals. I'm being my best self this weekend. I'm not making the same mistakes I always make. And this is the way to do it.

"Toni," I say, trying to project as much confidence and assured-ness as I can into my voice. I realize with a wave of awareness that I really need this. More than just a fun weekend with my bestie, I need to do something good for someone, and for myself. I need her to say yes.

"I think I can help."

TONI

FRIDAY AFTERNOON

"No."

I turn back to the tent to finish helping this girl and get back to whatever remains of my weekend. Now that I can't compete in the Golden Apple, this whole thing is barely more than another incoming college student getting a last hurrah before moving to campus. It feels cliché and empty and all the things I never wanted.

"Well, why not?" Olivia maneuvers around so she's directly in my line of sight and puts her hands on her hips. She cocks her head to the side like she has the audacity to be indignant. "You need me, and I just volunteered out of the goodness of my heart. I'm also a totally adequate singer. You should be saying thank you."

I lower my sunglasses so I can look at her without any tint coloring it. She's short, but her bun full of braids adds nearly a foot to her stature. Her face is perfectly made up, even despite the asthma/tent attack earlier, her round cheeks practically glowing. She's light skinned enough that I can already see the redness from an inevitable sunburn inching across her exposed shoulders. And even though her expression is currently twisted into a scowl, she's . . . cute. That's strike one.

"Because I don't do group work," I finally answer. "And I don't take favors."

I push my glasses back up and weave one of the aluminum poles through the tent's nylon. This whole interaction is slowing me down. That's strike two.

Maybe it was always meant to be this way. What kind of clarity was I supposed to get from a performance where I bombed? I haven't even managed to pick through an entire song for eight months. I've barely been able to stomach the thought of playing again since Dad's funeral. Why did I think coming here and entering this *X Factor* knockoff contest was going to help me decide what to do with my life? It was all a longshot anyway.

"But!" She huffs. "Remember back there when you saved my life? Those were good times, weren't they? We made some real memories, I'd say."

"Why are you pressing this so hard?" I stare at her.

I realize this is the longest conversation I've had with anyone that isn't my mom or Peter in longer than I can remember. I've only known this girl for thirty minutes and she's managed to blow past years and years of practice of saying the bare minimum and only when spoken to. That's strike three.

"Actually, don't answer. I don't need to know." I wipe my hands on my shorts and jerk my head toward her tent. This interaction being over is past due. "Have a good weekend."

I start in the direction of the Core and text Peter that I'm heading to him. My mind is whirring with everything not competing in the Golden Apple will mean. Adulthood is just a series of compromises. With no direction for the future, I spend four years at a college I don't want to attend. I graduate with a degree I don't care about and start a career that I stumble into and then I stick with it for forty years. My mom is proud because I've done the right thing, the stable thing, but before I know it, I've forgotten what it feels like to be seventeen and have *options*. Even if I have no idea what those options are, or how to pursue them.

I'm staring down the barrel of the rest of my life, and I don't like what it promises.

I instinctively walk a little faster, trying to go somewhere, anywhere I can escape my own fate.

"Wait!" I look over my shoulder and Olivia is running toward me. Or, well, running as well as she can given the way her chunky sandals are currently clomping against the wide gravel road that leads to the Core. When she reaches me, she immediately takes a hit of her inhaler and sighs. "What if it were a trade?"

I blink. "What?"

"You scratch my back, I scratch yours. Quid pro quo. My cart, your wagon. I've dated like four speech and debate kids, by the way, so I have a million of these euphemisms."

She's smiling, and it's bright and winning and if I were another type of person with a different type of damage, I'd probably be charmed. But I'm not. So as it stands, I'm just getting more and more frustrated.

"You don't make sense."

I keep walking, but she marches right alongside me. I've never seen someone so unwilling to be shaken, especially by me, except for maybe Peter. Normally it doesn't take much more than a look to keep people from sitting at my table in the cafeteria or trying to partner with me in AP Chem or sell me something on the street. There's a reason my classmates used to call me Mrs. Claus, and it's not because of my proclivity for cookie baking and rosy cheeks.

It's because I'm the ice queen. And I'm usually very good at it.

"I do make sense, Grumpy Gussie, you're just not paying attention," she says. "I'm saying we make this a trade. Then it's less like I'm doing you a favor and more like this is an even exchange. A meeting of the minds!"

I stop. I don't respond, and she takes that as her cue to continue with her proposal.

"Have you heard of #FoundAtFarmland?"

Of course. Of freaking course this girl wants help finding those stupid apples for that stupid scavenger hunt. I should have guessed. All Farmland newbies fall into the trap of trying to accomplish those promotional gimmicks. One year it's a social media campaign run by Live Nation to see who can add the most posts to their hashtag in exchange for a year's worth of free concert tickets. The next it's something even more obnoxious. And it's never about the music.

Past the fact that it's ridiculous, and honestly mortifying (my dad would roll over in his grave if he knew I was participating in some capitalist marketing scheme that used live music as a means to ply people into buying more and consuming more), it's also impossible. And I tell her so.

"This festival is on seven hundred acres of land. There's no way you'll find them all."

"It's not impossible for someone like you. Someone who knows this place as well as you must after so many years of being here." She shrugs. "If you need me just as badly as I need you, then you know I can't let you down. Right?"

She pushes her heart-shaped sunglasses into her hair and holds out a hand like it's already a done deal. Like her argument has been made and it was so undeniably effective I have no choice but to buy in.

And maybe she's right. What choice do I have? Without any other plans, I'm headed to Bloomington next week, no questions asked. I'll be the daughter my mom raised me to be, one who makes solid decisions and sticks to them. So unless I get on stage, and like my dad always said, it reveals another option, then college is it. That's how this works.

"I would really like to win that car." Olivia holds her hand up even higher and smiles even wider. "And I would like to help you win that competition. So, what do you say?"

I don't have any more strikes to spare, so I decide to wipe the slate clean. A fresh start.

I try to settle the screaming in the back of my brain telling me that this is a bad idea, that Toni Foster doesn't do this, that I can't do this, that I should not do this. That the more you rely on other people, the easier it is to get screwed over. I take her hand and do my best to ignore how her palm fits perfectly in mine.

"Fine." I shake once. "I'm in."

OLIVIA

FRIDAY AFTERNOON

When I leave Toni near the campsites to find Imani and catch her up on the change of plans for the weekend, I expect to see my best friend doing a lot of things. Maybe standing directly in front of a huge fan in the Core, trying to cool down from what she called "unconscionable heat" earlier. Or even grabbing a snack at that taco cart that everyone on the message boards said was a Farmland can't-miss food. I would have gone so far as to even say maybe she's found a band playing and is already enjoying a set.

I never would have expected her to be talking to a guy. And from what I can see, he's a *cute* guy!

"Olivia! Over here." She waves me closer once she stops me weaving through the crowd of people. It took me a surprisingly long time to get through security because they were so thorough, long enough that my best friend has been replaced with an unusually chipper clone.

When I get closer to the taco cart they're standing near—so she *did* end up eating at the taco cart!—the guy, who has to be around our age, smiles like I'm his long-lost buddy back from battle. I do a quick inventory: His curly black hair is tucked under an old baseball cap and his long, skinny brown arms remind me a little bit of those wobbly things from car dealership parking lots. He's basketball player tall, but with none of the solid athleticism that any of the basketball players I've dated have had. And he's wearing a crop top. With jorts.

It takes all of five seconds before I decide to claim him as my lanky cinnamon roll son.

He holds a hand up for a high five, which I immediately reciprocate. I'm nothing if not a sucker for an enthusiastic high five.

"Peter Menon, nice to meet you," he says. I look over at Imani and she kind of shrugs, like she's as confused as I am about why she's conversing with a stranger. It's not that Imani isn't social—she is. Just, usually only with people we already know. She's never been a huge fan of strangers. That's my territory. "Me and Imani were just bonding over the unusual spiciness of these things."

"You should have seen us. It was like that Paul Rudd *Hot Ones* meme."

They laugh at this tiny inside joke thing, but I don't blame them because who doesn't love Paul Rudd? I reach for the Fujifilm mini hanging around my neck to snap a picture of the two of them mid-snort. I shake it out and smile. Huh. Look at us.

"You guys have great energy," he says, still smiling. He snaps once. "Yo! You two should meet my friend. I'm getting ready to meet up with her over near the Farmland sign. She's signing up for the Golden Apple." He pulls his phone from his pocket and scrolls through it to get to his texts. "You two have to hear her voice! She's amazing."

I laugh a little at Peter's enthusiasm, his energy so palpable I feel like I'm absorbing it based on proximity alone. "Oh that's perfect, actually, because that's where we're headed."

I link my arm with Imani's and Peter air-drums as we walk.

Imani hates when I change plans last minute, so I try to ease her into it. I didn't think about her reaction when I decided to do this, and now I realize what an error in judgment that might be. She wanted a strictly best friend weekend, and this throws a slight wrench in the program. But! On the bright side, this could win me a car, which means Imani won't have to drive me everywhere all the time, and since I'm pretty much perpetually broke, she won't have to pay for that extra gas anymore. All I have to do is frame it like that and she'll practically be begging me to loop Toni into our weekend plans. It's pretty much a sure thing.

Pretty much being the operative words.

"So here's the deal, while you were gone I had this thing happen—"

"I've been working out a bit of an itinerary so we don't get off track," she interrupts, analytical and full speed ahead, as always. "I'm thinking we can ride the Ferris wheel now, maybe catch one of those local acts on the Red Delicious stage, and then check out some of the vendors."

I open my mouth to stop her, to slow her down just long enough for me to tell her about the scavenger hunt, but my phone buzzes over and over again. I think it might be urgent, but when I pull it out, there are messages from my mom populating the screen. The reminder of my lie, the only one I could have told to get out of her sight for a whole weekend, tastes bitter in my mouth as I read them. I don't want to use her God to get what I want, what I need, but there was no other way.

It's not like she trusts me anymore, after everything. It's not like she'll ever trust me again.

> Don't forget to give Imani gas money for driving you to the retreat.

> And make sure to pray before you eat. You always forget.

> This will be good for you.

It's the last text that does it, that makes me stumble a little as we walk. She might as well be thumping a bible right in front of my face. *This will be good for you* rattles around inside my brain until it's the only thing I can hear. There's so much bound up in those six little words. The ways I need to change, the way she thinks I need to do it. I'm too fast, too *loose*, too wicked for my own good. She's reminded me as much nearly every day since everything happened with Troy.

It's bad enough that my mom thinks I'm incapable of making good decisions—that all my best intentions end up getting people hurt. The worst part is that she's totally right.

I feel a fresh wave of purpose hit me. We're going to solve this scavenger hunt. I'm going to live up to my promise to Imani, get this car, have a great weekend, and leave this place—and Toni—somehow better than I found them. I can turn over a new leaf. I *can*.

"Imani, listen, before we do any of that, we've had a teensy itty-bitty tiny change of plans," I rush out. I want to explain before we get to Toni, and I'm running out of time. Imani's face contorts with confusion—which very rarely happens because Imani always, *always* has the answer.

Peter points to the sign with one hand and taps Imani's shoulder with the other. "There's my friend!" Imani looks to where he's pointing, and I can't help but follow Peter's finger as well. There are easily twenty people gathered around the sign right now, so it's hard to figure out who he means until he adds, "She's the one in the hat!"

Peter takes off in her direction—sprinting like a puppy off his leash—and it doesn't take long for me to realize who he was pointing to. When I spot her, my heart launches into my throat, and like, not in the fun roller coaster way. Of course this is how it works out. I try to ramble through the rest of my explanation quickly, but I know I'm not going quickly enough.

"You know how I was mentioning that I want to get a car? Well funny story, this girl I met—"

"How do you know Peter?" Toni says once we get within a few feet. Her voice is so succinct and her stare so hard, it's impossible to pretend like she's not talking to me.

Peter looks between Imani and Toni, excited but a little thrown. "Wait, you've met Imani?"

Imani unlinks her arm from mine and jerks her chin at Toni.

"No. How do *you* know Olivia?" she asks.

And, so quickly it's like they rehearsed it, they all look at me.

I hold my hands out to the side, palms up, the picture of a guilty woman.

"Um," I start, looking at all of them not so patiently waiting for an answer. "Hey, Farmers?"

TONI

FRIDAY AFTERNOON

I feel like I'm in the middle of an Old West showdown, and I'm not entirely sure, but I think I may have accidentally drawn my weapon first. When Olivia walked up with Peter and her friend, I just didn't know what to make of it. I never agreed to loop Peter into the plan, and I especially didn't factor in that this would become some sort of big collaborative effort. The thought of tangling this temporary thing with Olivia up into my permanent thing with Peter got my wires crossed.

"So I'm what? Just supposed to trot along after some girl I don't know all weekend?" Olivia's friend—Imani, I remember—crosses her arms over her chest and shoots daggers in my direction.

She didn't seem to like the explanation about the scavenger hunt, and my involvement in it, any more than I did. But somehow—and maybe credit is due here to Mrs. Robertson's note in my seventh grade report card to *Try not to withdraw when presented with new circumstances or people*—my reaction isn't to just walk away.

I start, "This obviously isn't what any of us thought—"

"Liv, if you want the car so bad, we can do this ourselves," Imani snaps. "I really don't think we have to do this follow-the-yellow-brick-road cosplay today."

Olivia's lips twitch like she's fighting back a smile, even as she nervously fiddles with the camera hanging around her neck. "Well, if I'm Dorothy, does that make you the Tin M—"

"Oh my God, Olivia, can you take anything seriously?" Imani throws her hands up and looks up at the sky.

This has gone far enough. If we're going to do this, get me on stage for the Golden Apple and win Olivia her scavenger hunt, then we need to get going. So I do something I never do in tense situations. I smile.

Peter shudders in shock, but Imani remains unmoved.

I kind of appreciate that about her. I never know what to do with wolves in sheep's clothing. If you're going to bite me, I want to see you coming.

I take a step forward and Imani leans toward Olivia, just slightly, like she's ready to shield her body with her own in case I try to do something to hurt her. It must be nice, having that type of connection with someone, where they'd be willing to trade their safety for yours if it meant you'd be protected.

Peter is great, and has been an annoying yet absolutely invaluable part of my life since I was eleven, but he lives on the opposite side of the country. While other girls I went to school with were going to the movies with their groups of best friends, having sleepovers that they live-posted about on Confidential, or posing refined and glamorous in manicured front yards before dances, I was at home, plucking out new riffs on my guitar. I was stumbling after my dad backstage at shows. I was choosing the safe route—the familiar route—shielding myself with music and solitude, rather than putting myself out there and trying to make friends my age.

Before I knew it, I was the ice queen—the girl too good to hang out. The girl too aloof to join in. Sure, it was a loneliness I chose, but that didn't make me any less alone.

So I feel a slight pang, always, at that type of loyalty. Sure, I watched those same girls get into fights and start drama and unfollow one another on Confidential, but a part of me still yearned for that. What it must feel like to care about someone enough to fight with them, to make up afterward? I didn't—don't—know.

"I think we should listen to her, you know? We've got a whole system planned out." Olivia squeezes Imani's arm gently. "Trust me."

She clearly doesn't trust me, but she's willing to trust Olivia, which is enough for right now.

"Here's what I'm thinking," I start.

I glance over at Olivia and she's looking back at me with an open expression, her lips curled up in a slight smile like she doesn't even know she's doing it. She reminds me a lot of my dad in that moment, the face he used to make when he was playing his old Gibson SG in the basement. A hope so still you don't want to move for fear of disturbing it.

"First things first: Everyone set their notifications to receive an update every time @FoundAtFarmland posts something. Cell reception out here gets spotty, and the last thing we need is for them to update and us not to be the first to see it," I say.

Peter is nodding along, his face attentive and waiting for instruction. It's a familiar look, one I've seen via FaceTime a million times since we became friends. Whatever he can do to help—to be needed—he's on board for.

I pull out my phone and motion to the first picture they posted an hour ago. According to their rules post, they'll be posting clues at random all weekend for five apples in total. They might already be collected by the time you arrive though, and if you're missing one you might as well be missing them all, so you have to move quick.

My heart is already beating like I'm a contestant on that chaotic reality show *The Amazing Race* or something. I don't even care about this stupid car, but winning suddenly feels hugely, ridiculously important. And we're already behind.

The first picture is the golden apple against a solid red background. It was clearly taken in the early morning, given the soft pinkish lighting, but it's shining with more than a flash. The whole photo has a cotton candy hue to it.

"And I think we need to split up. There are only two places I can think of where this would be."

I've been to Farmland so many times, there isn't a lot of ground I haven't covered over the past decade or so of my life. I send Peter and Imani off to check behind the Goldspur barn near the area with the food stalls, and I suggest Olivia and I head in the direction of the billboard—a low wall with a platform that illuminates the posters on it just like a billboard on the side of any highway. We get closer to it, and I can already tell that, as usual, it's currently plastered with posters about voter registration and reducing waste and schedules of the weekend's lineup.

It sits low enough to the ground that people also take the liberty of signing the back of it. They paint over it each year so the next group of Farmers can make it their own, but it's a Farmland tradition.

Olivia and I are moving quick, just in case someone else has the same idea as us. It made sense for us to split into teams with one person who'd been to Farmland before and one newcomer, and Peter was a little too eager to go to the other spot with Imani.

"Chicago is great for concerts, but the parking is always terrible, you know? Imani hates going up there because—Oh wait!" Olivia stops and holds the camera hanging around her neck up to her eye. It's one of those cute little pink ones you can buy at Urban

Outfitters, the ones that print out miniature vintage-looking photos right then and there. She points it straight ahead and clicks once. "Did you see that?"

She takes the printout and hands it over to me. It's still clearing, so I don't know exactly what she expects me to look at. She nods her head in the direction of the stage in front of us.

"That little kid on his dad's shoulders. See them?"

She's not looking at me, so I follow her eyes to the crowd gathering in front of the Granny Smith stage. A kid no older than four or five has his hands in the air and a pair of noise-canceling headphones on as he watches an indie band that I don't know play.

It's such an ordinary moment, but there's something beautiful in it. Especially when the dad looks up at his son and smiles. It's simple, but special. Memorable.

The picture doesn't quite capture what we're looking at in person, but I get why she wanted to freeze it in time. I wouldn't have thought about it, probably would have barely filed it away in the recesses of my mind, but Olivia thought to stop. To hold on to it.

I hand the photo back to her without saying any of that though.

"It's nice," I say instead.

"Nice." She smirks. She starts walking again. "You are a woman of few words, Toni. Can't relate!"

Then she giggles at her own observation, the sound of it almost cartoonishly high, and I smile, even though I don't want to. It's hard not to when she laughs like that. When we get closer to the billboard, it's clear that my guess was right. The apple sits nestled between slats in the wood platform, obscured just so by the over-sized light fixture that illuminates the billboard at night. An easy get since it's the first clue, no doubt.

Olivia brightens even more once we spot it.

"Oh my gosh, Toni, you were right!" She shoves at my shoulder playfully. "I have a nose for sniffing out good people. Well, okay, so I also have a nose that sniffs out people that seem good and then turn out to be pretty terrible, but in this case—"

"Um, Olivia." I hold my hand out to pause her rant and jerk my head to the side. A pair of girls in fairy wings and flower crowns seem to have the same idea as us. They move casually, laughing, coming from the opposite direction until one of them stops and straightens suddenly. Her eyes lock on mine and she points, just barely, at the two of us. "Do you have your inhaler?"

Olivia follows my line of vision straight to the fairy pair and freezes just for a second. She reaches down to pat her fanny pack, locates the L-shaped outline of her inhaler, and nods slowly.

"On three?" I ask. She nods again. The fairy girls are moving slowly in the direction of the apple, trying to psych us out, I'm sure, with their meandering steps. I start the count: "One, two—"

But Olivia is off like a bolt before I get the chance to hit three, sprinting through the crowd of people between us and the bill-board, shouting apologies all the way. I take that as my cue to do the same, and the minute I do, the fairies begin their own barefoot run. Their wings are offering just enough wind resistance to slow them down, so although they were closer, Olivia manages to get to the apple first.

She grabs it and holds it above her head, victorious.

"Toni! We got it!" she shouts in my direction. I stop and take a deep breath, trying not to smile. I want to feel relieved, but then I realize the fairies haven't stopped. In fact, as Olivia puts a hand on her knee to try and catch her breath, one of the fairies—the one with pink wings—reaches over and snatches it directly out of her other hand. Olivia looks up and wheezes between breaths, "Wha—wait! That's *totally* not in the Farmland spirit!"

But the fairy isn't listening, or stopping—she's ducking under the bottom of the billboard and taking off, her friend in tow. They're closer to me now than they are Olivia, who is fumbling for her inhaler. And that, if nothing else, is what kicks me into overdrive. It's bad enough that they violated the spirit of this festival by doing something dirty like stealing from a fellow Farmer, but to do it while she's fighting off an asthma attack?

That's a special kind of messed up.

As I head toward the fairy with the apple in hand, I bump into a burly shirtless guy carrying a totem with a light-up teddy bear on top and lose my footing. I fall directly in front of Pink Wings, and in some graceless act of mercy, she trips over my prone form. Her partner, Lime Green Wings, scrambles to pick up the apple that got dropped in the shuffle, crawling between the legs of all the people on the dirt path trying to get to the first sets of the day.

I lose track of it, and Olivia, until I hear her voice between barely successful attempts to get air into her lungs, "Try and"—wheeze—"take it"—wheeze—"from me now,"—wheeze—"Tink."

I scramble to my feet as Olivia shoves the apple into her fanny pack. The fairy on top of me flops to the side in defeat, and the fairy at Olivia's feet bangs a fist against the ground. The scene is absurd, strange, and oddly cinematic. I wipe my hand across my sweaty forehead and meet Olivia's eyes from across the pathway. When she beams with self-satisfaction, my chest swells with an emotion that feels a little too close to pride.

And this time I can't keep myself from smiling right back.

OLIVIA

FRIDAY AFTERNOON

I'm sweaty and gross and breathing hard and I'm not even embarrassed. And then there's Toni, smiling at me like I'm not a total mess. Deciding not to fall in love with her has given me a sense of freedom. It takes the pressure off, the edge that laces every conversation when you want someone to want you the same way you want them—that changes behavior and adds tension and just overlays every interaction with some level of performance.

My heart beats a little faster, and it isn't because of that daring apple rescue I just managed. When Toni smiles, and really means it, she looks a little like a Disney princess who stumbled onto the set of a Kittredge music video, and it's too freaking much, okay?

It's just not right. It should be illegal. It's just plain criminal, the way her eyes crinkle at the corners and she looks down at the ground like she's a little self-conscious about allowing herself a moment of happiness. I should call in a citizen's arrest. Someone has to get me away from her before I—

"Olivia!" Imani and Peter are suddenly in front of me and I'm not sure how they got there. Toni stands behind them, smile dimmed from the ridiculously breathtaking thing it had been just a few moments before. I want her to smile at me like that again.

Until I look at Imani's face and realize that her eyes have narrowed into slits. I've been clocked.

"So, you've got your apple. We can go now?"

She reaches out and wiggles her fingers like she wants me to take her hand and come with her. And I would, I totally would, but Toni's smile or not we still have four apples to find today, so we couldn't abandon the two of them even if I wanted to. And I don't want to. Not yet.

It's Peter who chimes in first though. "Well, don't we have to do this all day? I mean, another clue could drop any minute."

He looks around at the three of us quickly, but his eyes linger on Imani for a beat too long. It's imploring, the kind of gaze I know I've worn too many times over the course of my life. In that moment, if I were a cartoon character, a light bulb would be flickering to life above my head.

Imani doesn't understand why I'm such a hopeless romantic because she's never felt it. She doesn't know the flip of your

60

stomach when the girl you like walks into the room or the anxious rush that follows sending that "what are we?" text to your maybe-boyfriend. She's never loved anyone besides Davey Mack, and he doesn't count because celebrities never count (it's in the handbook—trust me, I wrote it). I've missed what was right in front of me: She's so easily annoyed by all my romances because she feels left out.

I kick myself for not realizing sooner—this could be another way for me to make things better for someone this weekend. Call me Jane Austen, because I'm about to *Emma* the hell out of Peter and Imani.

"We should go see the solo acts who are performing for the Golden Apple today," I say, clapping my hands together like a cheerleader. "I just got a notification from the Farmland app. They're starting now. We can go to the Cortland performance barn and get a sense of the talent. It'll be helpful for us"—I gesture between me and Toni—"and be a good way to kill time until the next clue."

All of which is true, but the most important part is that the performance barn equals a dark space with close seating. The perfect setup for a romantic scene between the two lovebirds.

Peter perks up immediately, his face and his floppy dark hair so hopeful in that moment that I have an overwhelming urge to just snuggle him. Imani clenches her outstretched hand into a fist and then releases it before sliding it into the pocket of her shorts. Toni shrugs like she couldn't care either way, and I try not to feel some type of way about that. This isn't about her. This is about Imani and Peter. (Until it's time to search for the next apple, in which case it will then be about me again. But whatever.)

"Fine," Imani huffs. Peter whoops and pumps one fist in the air. Part of me is convinced the guy has never experienced a bad mood in his life, he's so happy.

He and Toni fall into step together and start in the direction of the performance barn, and Imani lowers her voice so that only I can hear as we follow.

"So how long do we have to deal with Thing One and Thing Two?" she asks. "I'm already annoyed with the Zoë Kravitz wannabe. Honestly, who does she think she is with that hat on?"

Imani's generally a curmudgeon, so her comment doesn't surprise me, but it does chafe a little. I mean, Toni might not be the most personable girl at Farmland, but she's been cool to me so far. Nice even. And she hasn't once asked me to be quiet, which is more than I can say for most people within ten minutes of meeting me. I feel the urge to defend her.

"I like the hat." I try to change the subject quickly. I elbow her gently. "But Peter is cute, right?"

"I don't know," she says with an eye roll so severe only she could do it. "I don't pay attention to that stuff. That's your domain, remember?"

I know she's joking, but my neck heats, embarrassed. I shouldn't have to feel bad about liking to kiss people and be kissed, but sometimes I really do. Sometimes, in moments when a person I love criticizes my penchant to go heart-first into everything I do, I realize there's nothing I should want to be *less* than a teenage girl who feels too much.

It's been a long time since the two of us fought. Like really, really went at it. So her reaction catches me off guard. I almost want to call the whole thing off; just apologize to Toni for agreeing to do this in the first place and stick with my initial plan of blowing off steam all weekend before the inevitable. Because in a few days, there will be a judicial hearing where the fate of Indiana's number one basketball recruit rests in my hands, and I have no intention of being there.

And when I tell Imani the truth, that I can't do it, I won't be surprised if she's too disappointed in me to even try and convince me to do the right thing anymore. That's how you know Imani has given up on you—when she doesn't even care enough to argue with you. But I have no choice. If I face the entire school board and tell them what happened between me and Troy from my perspective, I will ruin his life—and my own in the process.

I try to push the thought out of my head, but I can't seem to shake it completely. My chest gets tight against my will.

"I don't want to talk about either of them," she says. She shakes her head and her long, loose wave bundles sway easily, kind of like she's as disinterested in getting into it here as I am. "This is a best friend weekend. Me and you." She adjusts her tortoiseshell sunglasses and raises her eyebrows. "Remember?"

I do remember. Of *course* I remember.

Imani and I didn't become friends because we both love the same movies or shop at the same stores or crush on the same celebrities. Our older siblings dated practically from the moment they started at Park Meade together. Nia and Wash. Valedictorian and salutatorian, Most Likely to Succeed and Most Likely to Be President, Harvard and MIT, respectively. Twin superstars of charm and charisma and good old-fashioned Black Excellence. It was no surprise they found each other. And no surprise me and Imani found each other as a result.

When you know what it's like to be second-best in your family, I think it's almost inevitable that you find the only other person who really gets it to make you their number one.

This wasn't something we talked about often, or ever really. But it was enough to build a truly iconic best friendship. Because as different as we are, we're the same in the ways that count. The ways that no one can quantify. It's why I listen to her in moments like this, even when I don't quite agree with her.

The look she gives me now though tells me everything I need to know. It tells me exactly why I can't bail on her for Toni, why I have to keep my eyes on the prizes: winning the scavenger hunt, competing in the Golden Apple tomorrow, and helping my best friend get one step closer to having an epic weekend romance with a cute—if a little goofy—boy she'll never have to see again.

I don't say anything else for the rest of the walk to the barn where the solo performances are being held. They're between acts, so there's a low hum of the audience talking and an empty stage with one light shining directly down on a lone microphone.

The barn is big, but not overly so. There are about 150 seats in the room, with a balcony with just enough room for a table and three judges. I can't make out their faces with the lights down so low, but I get excited anyway. Whoever they are, they're *famous*. I'm not too cool to admit that the thought of being in the room with someone who may or may not have met Beyoncé is pretty much earth-shakingly impressive, okay?

The four of us file down the aisle to a row in the back with vacant seats. We're getting ready to step into the row when I realize the order is all off. It's Peter, me, Imani, and then Toni. That defeats the entire purpose! At the last second before we step into our row, I reach for Peter.

"Peter, I'm so sorry, would you mind swapping seats with me? I'm so short, it's easier for me to see if I'm closer to the middle."

It's a totally nonsense excuse, honestly a hail Mary, but Peter nods so quickly his baseball cap almost flies off his head.

"Of course!" He brightens so fast it's like he was just looking for a way to make himself more useful. "Did you know the shortest US president was around your height? James Madison clocked in at a whopping five-four. I've always thought it was unfair when people can't, like, reach the top shelf and stuff. This is practically height reparations." I groan and laugh at the same time at the terrible comparison.

"Reparations isn't the word you want to use with three Black women, Pete," Toni mumbles. She sits down with a huff and slides her sunglasses off her eyes and into the collar of her tank top. She sighs and pinches the bridge of her nose. "Know your audience, remember? We've talked about this."

Peter's eyes go wide. But I wave off the apology that's coming. That move probably lost him a couple points with Imani, but I think we can get them back if he just keeps his foot out of his mouth.

"Wow! Can't wait for the next act!" I say, overly loud, trying to pivot away from the awkward situation that threatens to descend if I let it. I plop down and Peter follows suit. And right on time too, because as soon as we're settled, the lights go down and the emcee steps out on stage to announce the next artist.

I chance one look over at Imani, who is staring back at me with a terrifying glare. I know she's annoyed that Peter and Toni are with us at all, but she'll understand it was for her own good one day. She can't see the forest because she's looking at the trees, or something like that. The next artist up is a white guy who looks like he can't be much older than us—probably a junior or senior in college. He steps onto the stage with nothing but a ukulele in his hand and adjusts the mic so it's level with his mouth. I don't really listen to his introduction; I think he says something about covering a song by Sonny Blue, but when Toni shifts out of the corner of my eye, I can't help but look over at her. Her eyes are locked so intently on the stage, it's mesmerizing.

She's focused on his every move, her expression all intense musician's attention. I imagine what she's going to look like when we play this stage tomorrow, if she's going to chance a look at the judges or play to the audience or if we'll simply watch each other. Like some kind of Black Sonny and Cher.

I'm lost in my thoughts, in imagining tomorrow's performance, when she stands up so fast she looks almost surprised at herself. It's like she doesn't even see the guy on stage, see anybody, anymore. And she walks out the door without a word.

TONI

FRIDAY AFTERNOON

I lean against the side of the barn and I press my hand to my chest as if that'll make the feeling in my heart go away. It's beating practically out of time, its intensity too much for me to take.

The guy on stage was playing every note correctly, singing adequately, but it wasn't *right*. He didn't understand the song, not really. His voice didn't have the rawness it's supposed to have to tell that story. He was close to the notes but too far away from the story—light where it should have been dark and quirky where it should have been gritty. My throat gets tight at the thought of the first time I heard this song.

I feel like I'm inside the moment Dad played it for me in his old pickup on our way to Farmland five years ago. I'd just said, "I don't think I like boys like I'm supposed to." And he'd responded, "Ain't no *supposed to*. When Bonnie Harrison wrote: *I'll face the thunder, the earth won't swallow me whole* it sure wasn't because she thought loving her wife was gonna be easy. Loving's not something you do because everybody thinks it's right—you do it 'cause hearts are all we got. Listen to this." And then he slid Sonny Blue's first CD into the truck's old CD player.

I'm suddenly overwhelmed with all the things I'll never get to share with him again. All the songs, all the memories, all the years we'll miss.

I breathe slowly, in and out. In and out. I try to focus on the now. On the way the heat warms my skin even in the shade of the barn, on the sound of sandals crunching across dry blades of grass nearby.

"Toni?" Olivia's voice is surprisingly soft as she walks around the edge of the barn and finds me. I look up, and for a moment I'm thrown by how strange it is to be approached with so much casual familiarity. In that second, I forget that I barely know this girl. "Peter wanted to come and see about you, but I told him I would handle it." She leans a shoulder against the wall so she's facing me. She smiles. "I think him and Imani are meant to be together."

I swallow down the lump in my throat and hope she can't hear how close I was to tears just ten seconds ago. "You think?"

"You betcha." She shoots the most enthusiastic finger guns I've ever seen at me. "I'm kind of a genius at these sorts of things." She pauses for a second and then amends herself. "I mean that I am good at the getting together part. The rest of it, not so much."

It sounds like there's a story there, but I'm not sure she really wants to tell it, and I definitely don't know if I want to hear it. I mean, we don't really know each other. And that's a good thing. I don't need any more complications this weekend than I already have. I mean, look at me. I heard a mediocre cover of a song that came out fifteen years ago and I practically imploded.

I'm unraveling.

"You left pretty fast, so you didn't see the end of that guy's performance. One of his strings snapped at the beginning of the last chorus." She shakes her head sadly. "I really felt for him. He's probably gonna be so down on himself for the rest of the weekend, you know?"

The poor guy probably didn't stand much of a chance anyway, given the pure odds of the thing, but I don't think that's the point. I hear what she's saying. Even if the deck was stacked against him, he lost his one shot because of something outside his control. You don't get over something like that easily, even if your better self tries to make sense of it. We want to believe our best try will be enough, and sometimes that's just not how it works.

Peter stumbles around the corner, all flailing long limbs and a cartoonish slide like he's running away from the villain in an episode of *Scooby-Doo*, and slides to a stop in front of the both of us. Imani rounds the corner much slower, arms crossed and eyes shooting daggers at everyone involved.

"Guys." Peter hurries to unlock his phone and holds it out in front of us.

On his screen there's a heavily filtered Instagram photo with a white girl with dreadlocks (a crime against my sensibilities for which someone should have to pay) smiling broadly while holding up a golden apple. *Our* golden apple. The caption says: "Looky what I found! Did I win?"

"I think we have some competition."

OLIVIA

FRIDAY AFTERNOON

I don't know how this girl got her hands on my apple, but I know very quickly that she is my nemesis and I want nothing more than to take her down. She is standing between me and my car, and that's simply not an option.

Not to mention, you lose this scavenger hunt and Toni has no reason to keep you around anymore. The deal is null and void, my ridiculous lizard brain reminds me. *If you're not good for a good time, then what use are you?*

I work my jaw, grinding my teeth together like I used to when I was younger. Before I realized that there was power in the way I could use my body to bend people to my will, to get them to *see me*, even if it was only the me I wanted them to see in that moment. It's a nervous habit that comes rushing back in moments of stress.

"How, pray tell, did this girl manage to find an apple that we hadn't even gotten a clue for yet?" Imani's hands are on her hips and she's pointing at the phone in Toni's hand like she somehow planned this. "Aren't you supposed to be the mastermind here?"

Toni looks between the two of us, trying to piece something together, and I look away. For some reason, having her eyes on me is even tougher to process than when she's vaguely distant, and I so don't know how to deal with that.

"Well, they never said they'd be putting the apples out as we went along. They just said they'd be dropping new clues throughout the weekend," she says, voice low and considering. "So, technically they're always in play."

"So, what do we do?" I ask.

She just stares at me for a beat before huffing out a breath. "It means that we have to get the apple back from this girl."

Peter brightens at that, even though he must have known that was the solution. He pulls out his phone and opens up the girl's Instagram page. @FestyFrankie has twenty-five thousand followers and has been updating every couple hours with different shots of her in various poses around the grounds. A wide stance and double peace signs with the Ferris wheel in the background. Blowing a kiss at the camera near the entrance, flower crown wrapped around her head.

It's easy to follow her whereabouts. Five minutes ago, she added a picture of a funnel cake to her story with the typewriter font in all caps saying SO YUMMY.

Toni rolls her eyes at that update, like the funnel cake has personally offended her sensibilities. I snort out a laugh. When I do, she snaps her head up to mine, a little surprised. But her lips tick up at the corners in a smile and it feels like a victory. Like a well-earned win against her general standoffishness.

"There are what? No more than three vendors who sell funnel cakes out here, according to this map."

Imani has pulled out the map that they gave us at check-in and is already running through a revised game plan. She's always been a take-charge type of person, the voice of reason, but another part of me wishes that I was the one with the answers this time. That it was my word dictating how everyone should handle this.

Peter beams and Toni nods. I make a suggestion: "Yeah, you're right. So, let's split up. Peter and—"

Imani interrupts. "Peter can take the booth by the entrance. Toni can take the one near the Comedy Pavilion. And me and Liv can take the one around the back."

I'm usually grateful for her interference, for her ability to spot when I'm getting ready to make a mistake before I can, but now I'm just . . . frustrated. Maybe I wouldn't have chosen to pair off with Toni. But I guess we'll never find out. It's like she's taking the choice out of my hands completely, not even giving me the opportunity to prove that I can do what I said I would do. That I won't jump at the first girl who bats her eyes at me or whatever.

"Okay. Yeah, okay." Toni looks between the two of us again, but this time her expression goes a little blank, a little hard. "We'll split up, and when one of us has eyes on her, we'll all text the group. Then we can figure out what comes next."

"Pop Top is going on in thirty," Peter says, looking at Toni imploringly. He makes prayer hands. "She literally reinvented pop punk—you know I can't miss my girl Pop Top."

Toni gently smacks the back of her hand against Peter's arm and rolls her eyes. "We better move fast then, Menon."

It's a quick moment, but the way she looks at him and he looks back, I get why two such different people are friends. They balance each other out and love each other all the same.

Imani huffs next to me and starts in the opposite direction, already in motion. It feels like Imani is always moving away from people while I'm rushing toward them, but we're both constantly in motion. As I turn to follow her, I wonder how long that type of opposite momentum can sustain itself.

I know Festy Frankie the minute I see her. Mostly because, well, I notice her dreads.

Festy—or Frankie? FF, maybe?—is still sitting on the ground between the funnel cake booth and the Granny Smith stage when I spot her. She giggles at something one of her friends says and then purses her lips and leans her head to the person next to her to pose for a selfie. Which, not to be a Boomer about it or anything, kind of annoys me. You stole my apple *and* you're not even paying attention to the band on stage? How dare!

Imani groans next to me like she can read my mind.

"You want to take this one or should I," she asks.

I think about the number of white girls Imani has read for filth on Confidential for everything from cultural appropriation to white feminism over the course of our friendship and shake my head. It's probably better if I take this one myself if I want any chance of us getting it back. You catch more white girls with honey than with vinegar, or however that saying goes.

"I'll handle it," I answer. "Wait here."

"Excuse me." I try to pitch my voice just slightly higher than it naturally is so me and Festy become one in the same. I don't know her, but I go to school with a hundred of her kin—the code switch is almost second nature to me now. "Are you @FestyFrankie?"

Frankie looks up at me and beams, her eyes hidden behind a pair of round John Lennon sunglass frames. I know from my time lightly stalking her page that she wore that same pair to Electric Forest back in June, and to Stagecoach last spring.

Despite the shades, she still puts a hand over her brow line to shield her from looking directly into the sun as she stares up at me. "Yes! Are you one of my lovely Festimals?"

Festimals. Festival animals. The nickname she has for her followers who attend festivals with the same amount of vigor she does. I have to give her credit—she's got a strong sense of branding. But that's not why we're here!

"No. Well, I mean, not exactly. I did see your post about the golden apple though? The one for the #FoundAtFarmland challenge?"

"Isn't it great?" She stands up, and like magic, produces the apple. She holds it in her left palm and pets it absently with her right much as if it were a small dog. "It was the craziest coincidence! I was trying to take a picture near the fountain and there it was, just waiting for me!"

I internally roll my eyes. *Give it a rest, Festy!* I don't have time to chat her up about this. I have a festival to get back to and a scavenger hunt to finish, all before I can even begin to think about how I can help Toni win the Golden Apple competition tomorrow. Diplomacy is key here.

"Are you searching for the rest of them?" I ask.

"Nope!"

She brightens like she doesn't have a care in the world. And, yeah, maybe I'm judging, but from the looks of her, she probably doesn't. She gets to go to festivals all year and make money being an Instagram influencer, selling God knows what. I saw at least one ad for flat tummy tea on her page. Whatever background she comes from, all I know is that I definitely need that apple more than she does.

"Could I borrow it from you then?" I rush out, trying to explain the situation. "I really need it to win the scavenger hunt it's attached to. I have a really good shot at getting the rest of them, but need the one you have to make it work. I can give it back when the weekend is over, even, if that—"

"Sorry, love. I collect Mementos." She says mementos with a capital M, like it's a proper noun that deserves to stand on its own and everything.

"I'm sorry, *what*? You can't let me borrow it, even though you don't actually need it, because it's going to go in some kind of memory box once you get back home?"

She nods seriously, pleased that I seem to be understanding. "Yes, exactly."

"But I'll bring it back. If it's important to you, I'll give it back once this is over."

"I'm sorry, my friend. I just can't bear to part with it."

She reaches out and pats my shoulder gently. If I weren't so annoyed, I imagine it would've been fine. I probably could have grinned through it, bit my tongue, and gone back to lick my wounds for the rest of the weekend—this part of the adventure over. But to say that would've been also giving up on the Golden Apple competition, and Toni. To say that would be to wave her off, to never see her again after just getting to meet her.

And a part of me I can't explain is just not ready for that.

So, I do what any rational person would do: I steal it. But not like those Tinkerbells tried to steal my apple from me earlier, obviously. I at least tried to come to a mutually beneficial agreement first. I was practically a diplomat about it!

I reach out and grab the apple from her hands so fast if I hadn't done it myself, I wouldn't have even realized I'd done it. One blink and the apple has gone from her hand to my fanny pack, and I'm booking it. I swing my camera to my back so it thumps against my shoulder blades as I run. While two dramatic escapes in one day doesn't come close to matching my record—summer after sophomore year got a little crazy, don't ask—it is killing my lungs!

I make a mental note to thank Justin for those three weeks I spent helping him train for varsity cross-country tryouts (after which we'd make out in his older brother's Ford Fusion before he drove me home for dinner).

"Imani, come on!" I shout as I pass her, and she takes off with me.

I'm dodging the bodies that have gathered in the Core, trying to make my getaway seem as innocuous as possible, despite the fact that @FestyFrankie is calling out behind me, her voice getting more and more faint as I dash toward the other side of the Core. But, given the amount of drugs people are no doubt going to get into this weekend, my behavior certainly isn't the strangest anyone will encounter.

My lungs are burning by the time I double over near the Red Delicious stage, clear across the Core from where we found Festy. It's only once I stop that the ridiculousness of what I've just done washes over me—the absolutely unhinged quality of *stealing a golden apple* from someone. My heart beats a little faster at the realization that I really have lost my mind. I've completely snapped.

I take a puff of my inhaler and my mind starts whirring sud-denly, and it's so fast it feels like my whole body is buzzing. Wait.

I'm *literally* buzzing.

I reach into my back pocket and grab my phone, and do my best to gather myself before sliding my thumb across the home screen to answer.

"No luck over here. What's the 411 on your side, O-Town?" Peter's voice is its normal mixture of peppy and raspy as it crack-les through the line.

I look at Imani, where she's doubled over next to me, glaring at me and then the ground and then me again like she can't figure out who to be annoyed with. I reach down to run a hand over my fanny pack where it bulges with the pilfered goods. I did it. I actu-ally did this. Not Imani, not Toni—I got this one and I did it all by myself.

I can't remember the last time that happened. I didn't have to rely on anybody to get this done. This victory is mine and mine alone. It's such a small thing, but it feels so huge in that moment.

A smile breaks across my face.

"I've got the apple."

TONI

FRIDAY AFTERNOON

When Olivia returns, shaking the apple triumphantly in our direction, Peter high fives her and I just stare. She tells us the story, a daring feat that involves her trying to negotiate with and then subsequently outrunning Festy Frankie, and she sounds so proud. And rightfully so. What she's managed to do already today, in pursuit of this car, has been impressive. *She's* impressive, and I'm not really sure what to make of it.

It's not that I'm never wowed by other people—it happens all the time: Teela Conrad showing off her five-octave vocal range, listening to Chuck Berry's lick in the intro to "Johnny B. Goode," watching Rihanna anytime she so much as breathes—it's just that I can usually school my reactions into something indecipherable. There's something about Olivia though that makes it hard to be impassive. I don't know why or how this girl is slipping past the barbed-wire fence and into the land of people I want to open myself up to, but I don't like it. I don't like it at all.

I keep my mouth shut as she and Peter do some kind of victory dance and I try to focus on the task at hand.

Peter turns to the group after the two finish their dance and holds his hands out wide. "Time to see the icon that is Pop Top."

We all stop at the hydration station to fill up our water bottles for the eighth time in less than eight hours. My limited-edition Farmland S'well hasn't seen this much action since this festival last year. The sun is inching its way across the sky, on its way to setting, but it doesn't feel that way. It feels like trying to breathe through a straw as we make our way through the crowd toward where Pop Top is set to perform.

Despite the humidity, this is my favorite kind of scene at Farmland: the festival coming to life. The first day is full of newer and more indie artists, and the crowd always takes a while to fill out. But by the late afternoon, the whole place begins to hum with excitement. The food and merch vendors in the Core are fielding increasingly longer lines, Farmers are still bounding with the type of energy you have before you've spent three days in near-sweltering heat and the reality of being back home settles into your bones. The knowledge that for the next few days you have a place you belong.

It's probably rose-colored glasses, or the fact that I was raised to trust in the magic of live music spaces, but even the fact that I'm Black and surrounded by mostly white people becomes less of an issue than usual. We weave through throngs of people, being greeted with the traditional "Hey, Farmer!" wave, and it's like wading out into the ocean for the first time: a bigness made even more expansive once you're enveloped in it, made a part of it.

It breaks my heart that I can't share this with my dad one more time. It makes me love him even more for introducing me to this place.

Despite how good I feel here though, I can't help but think about my mom's warning before I left this morning: *"Be safe. You never know what people are capable of."* It's only been five years since that shooting at the nightclub in Orlando, four since all those people were killed at that festival in Vegas. Two years since that racist murdered all those people in that Walmart in Texas. The list goes on.

She was right to be cautious about coming to a place like this, I know. These days, the danger of just being alive and in public is practically as American as fireworks on the Fourth or apple pie or voter suppression. But this. *This* is what it's all about.

You take your chances going to the movies or out to eat or to a concert because this is what it feels like to be alive. Feeling the stifling late-summer air blanketing your limbs, people you care about around you, music you love playing nearby and reminding you why you love it.

We wind our way into the crowd in front of the Honeycrisp stage, bodies pressing in on all sides. Like always, my skin feels alight with anticipation as we wait for the set to begin—my first show of the festival. The girl next to us is wearing a shirt with Pop Top's logo, and the guy behind us is holding a sign that says POP TOP, WILL YOU MARRY ME? She's not a superstar yet, but she's on her way to it. Pop-punk outfits fronted by neon-green-Afro-having Black women are few and far between. She's impossible to ignore.

When Pop Top takes the stage, her band behind her, the crowd immediately erupts into chaos. And without so much as an introduction, her guitarist launches into the jarring and iconic single-note intro to her first radio hit, "Flowergirl."

"This is amazing!" Olivia shouts in my direction as the people in front of us start pushing back to form that telltale circle for a mosh pit. Peter is absolutely losing his mind as Pop Top gets to the first verse, and his enthusiasm is matched by the crowd around us. "Everything is so . . ."

She waves her hand around and she doesn't have to explain. I know exactly what she means.

The audience explodes when Pop Top launches into the chorus—a return to early-aughts emo that has everyone around us shoving one another, bursting uncontained like a bottle that's been shaken up and finally uncorked. It never stops being incredible, seeing hundreds of people move together in this way.

I look to my left, and Olivia is into it, bobbing her head along and mouthing the words like this scene is nothing new to her, but it's Imani that surprises me. For the first time since I met her, she throws herself into the music, and into the crowd, matching Peter's energy blow for blow.

Me and Olivia make it for the first fifteen minutes of the set before the two of us need a break. I'm sweating in the worst way and she's breathing a little too hard, so I grab the tapestry from Peter's backpack and take it to the grass behind where the last of the Pop Top fans are. I spread it out and Olivia immediately kicks off her shoes. She wiggles her toes and leans back to stare up at the sky.

"I love this place," she says, smiling toward the sun.

"Yeah," I say. I catch myself staring before she opens her eyes, and I look away quickly. "The feeling, um, never changes."

"That's one of my favorite parts about concerts, you know?" She turns to lay on her side and props her head up on one arm. "It's like being part of some, I don't know, organism? A living thing. All of us part of a body that needs full participation from each cell to function. You know what I mean?"

I was only adequate at science in school, but I understand what she's saying.

"Yeah, exactly. The bands are the lungs, but we're the breath."

She opens her mouth to respond but pulls her phone out instead. She starts typing furiously.

"*We are the breath that gives purpose to your lungs. This movement, your body's greatest gift,*" she says once she's finished. Her smile is shy, a little abashed for the first time since we met. "It's just—I do this thing online. Small lines with snapshots I've taken. Kind of like my concert diary, only I share it with the world? I don't know, it sounds kind of stupid when I explain it but . . ."

Maybe it's how resigned she is to that word, or how quickly she dialed her enthusiasm back, like someone has told her to be less of herself before, but I'm suddenly filled with an urge to contradict her.

"Can I see it?" I ask. It doesn't sound stupid at all, and as she hands it over, I know with full certainty just how not stupid it is. "You're a writer. That's impressive."

"No, oh my God, no! I'm not. Not really. I just want to catalog everything? I don't want to lose these feelings and these moments, and I don't know, it just feels like scrapbooking has gone the way of the dinosaurs and LiveJournal is a thing I only know about from Tumblr so—"

"That looks like a lyric." I stop her. I don't want her to second-guess herself. I hand her phone back and scratch the back of my neck. "It's hard to do that. You're good."

The words feel unfamiliar as they tumble out of my mouth, but I can't seem to stop them. I try to keep myself from slipping any further into dangerous territory—that space where winning the

Golden Apple and finding my Truth is no longer the most pressing thing in my life—and I'm worried I'm failing.

"Well, thank you? I guess. I just—It's not going to be a *career* or anything, it's just something to pass the time, so I try not to put too many eggs in that basket, you know? It's fun and everything, but—"

"Olivia."

"Hm?"

"Have you ever taken a compliment without explaining your way out of it?"

She huffs out a laugh and focuses her eyes on a random spot on the tapestry.

"You, um, can. With me," I say. I wait until she looks at me again before adding, "Take them, I mean. I wouldn't lie to you."

And I know I say it kind of seriously, but I want her to know that about me. I believe all we have is our word, that when we say things we should mean them, and mean them wholeheartedly. I know from experience how much empty statements and promises with no follow-through can pull a person apart, piece by piece. I wouldn't do that to her.

"I—" she starts, and then shuts her mouth. "I don't usually get a lot of compliments for being like this." She laughs a little. "I'm much better at playing the version of myself other people expect."

My stomach flips. Part of me wants to reach for her. The part that's always sort of been there, buzzing, begging to hold or be held. But I don't do that. I can't be that kind of person.

So I grab her camera where it sits on the tapestry next to us and snap a picture of her profile as she looks at the crowd in front of us. The sun gives her face a glow, like it rises to meet her in the morning and not the other way around. The snap is enough to get her to look at me again, but this time her expression is different than any I've seen on her before. It's contemplative, a little reserved. She takes the photo where it dangles from the camera and shakes it out a bit.

"Here," she says, after it clears. "Something to remember me by when this is all over." She smiles a little as she tucks it into my open fanny pack. "Submit it to galleries and call it *Aftermath of Cute Girl's Compliment*. You'll get rich for sure."

I don't have a response to that—don't even know how to begin to make sense of the moment we just had. So I pretend to listen to Pop Top. I try to ignore the feeling that I'm sinking into something here that I don't have the tools to fight.

And the fact that maybe I don't want to.

OLIVIA

FRIDAY AFTERNOON

"I want to go to the Ferris wheel." Odd Ones, the band that took the stage after Pop Top finished, have just wrapped up their encore, and now Imani is standing over me with her arms crossed and her face saying that this isn't a request, it's a demand. I should have known that sitting out two sets in a row wouldn't bode well with her. I look at Toni—not for permission, just to, like, excuse myself—and she says, "I should go check on Peter. He's like a succulent—he can survive alone for a while, but he does better when someone is tending to him."

I brush myself off and follow Imani.

She moves a little too fast for a while, until we're out of the range of Toni and Peter and the last set we saw. She's shockingly athletic for someone who spent most of junior year eating lunch in the library in order to maximize her study time. I have to dodge people lying out in the grass, and skip over the corners of blankets to keep up with her as she moves. The Ferris wheel lights up in the distance, massive and glittering and colorful, and I have the urge to take a picture. But I decide to wait until the sun goes down instead.

I give the "Hey, Farmer" wave to a couple as I pass and they wave back, and it's just so *nice*. It's so easy.

And I realize that even though I'm covered in a thin layer of sweat and I can already feel some particularly heinous tan lines brewing and I've drunk more water over the course of the past few hours than I ever have before, I'm content.

For the first time in months, I've gone nearly an hour without thinking about the hearing. I'm not thinking about toppling my next conquest—honestly, I'm not even thinking about finding the next apple. I'm settled in my skin. It's so unfamiliar to me though, I almost don't recognize it for what it is. But I'm me, so of course it doesn't last for long.

"You should be careful," Imani says, stepping over the legs of a guy in a Kittredge T-shirt. He waves at her as we pass, but I don't think she notices.

"I already told you I was wearing SPF 30," I say, trying to joke my way out of the tone she's using. "I read something that says once you go too far over it doesn't actually work."

"You know I'm not talking about that." We stop in front of the Ferris wheel, and she looks over at the way my shoulders are reddening. "You do need a reapplication, but I'm talking about this." She waves her hand around easily, gesturing at everything.

I tell myself Imani just wants what's best for me, wants a future where the people who have broken my heart get broken in some way in return. But that's because she doesn't see me for what, for *who*, I am. That part of me probably deserves the heartbreak. I'm a one-woman wrecking crew and eventually I destroy the people closest to me, especially the people I decide to love.

At some point, I got really good at the chase. I got so good at it that most days, most nights, I barely even had to try. It became second nature, putting on a costume and becoming who I needed to become to get the attention of someone smarter, funnier, more talented than me. And I'd be able to hold their attention for a while. But pieces of me would inevitably begin to slip out. I'd talk too much about the wrong things, go overboard with a display of affection, or worse.

Cal, the debate team captain, said I distracted him away from his shot at state when I showed up in a brand-new bright orange jumpsuit I discovered at a garage sale. Moira, star forward for the girls' soccer team, sprained her ankle the night before sectionals because I insisted on going to the skating rink for our two-month anniversary. I wore this great pair of thrifted Saint Laurent velvet platform sandals to Kai's Battle of the Bands performance, but tripped and fell into their kit, effectively destroying their lucky cymbal five minutes before curtain. And then there was Troy.

They all ended the same way. In flames.

The only relationship I haven't ruined is this one, our friendship.

"I know you came here to have a getaway, but you've had months to figure out what you're going to say at the hearing, and you still refuse to tell me," she says. Her voice gets a little quiet. "Since when do we keep secrets from each other?"

I kinda want to stomp my foot like a toddler having a temper tantrum because *Oh my God.* I don't want to do this today. I don't want to do it any day.

It's incredible how fast all the warmth that I'd felt just ten minutes earlier, lying in the grass with Toni, disappeared. One reminder of my latest and greatest screwup, the last relationship that self-destructed as a result of my own poor decision-making, and it's like being splashed with cold water. Only worse because I'm drowning in my own shame.

"Imani, please." I can hear the whine coming through my voice and I have to turn to my last resort. I put on my best doe eyes. And because I don't know what else to do, I lie. "I'm not keeping anything from you. Can we just focus on the weekend?"

I don't know when the switch flipped, when our relationship became this weight where I feel like a burden to her too. The same way I do around my mom, or Nia—like I'm this defective thing beyond repair—but I don't like it. I don't understand it. If there's one person I've always known I could count on to love me despite all my wrongness, it would be her.

"You're not—" She stops walking and turns to me right before we reach the ticket booth. "You're not, you know, trying to hook up with Toni, right?" She twists the silver ring around her pinky. We bought it at Navy Pier during a weekend trip to Chicago last year to get over my breakup with Brianna, the drum major for the marching band. We had a matching set until I lost mine during a late-night swim in Theodore from Theater's pool. "Because you promised this would be just us."

My heart pangs hard and sudden.

"I meant it." I shake my head, just grateful that she doesn't hate me. That she hasn't been so relentless recently because she's ready to toss me to the curb. "We pinky swore on it," I add.

I throw my arms around her neck and hold her tight. I tuck my face into the space between her neck and shoulder and she brings her arms up to wrap around my back. She feels so solid, like always. My best friend, the lighthouse in the worst storm.

"I love you, Mani." My voice is muffled by her shirt. "You're always looking out."

"I love you too," she says, voice quiet. When we pull back, she sighs softly, exhausted, no doubt by the ridiculous sun and the Georgia humidity.

Her eyes skate across my face briefly and she shakes her head. She waits a second before saying, "Wash hated heights when we were kids. We'd go to the state fair every year, and my parents would never let me do the Ferris wheel because he couldn't do it. They didn't want him to 'feel bad.'" She puts air quotes around her words and looks at me with a half-smile (because a full one might just cause her to pull a muscle). I smile back twice as wide. "This is like a lifetime in the making. You should write this down for posterity."

I look up at the Ferris wheel, where the lights dance purple and pink across the late afternoon sky. Big, bold, its presence inescapable. I hold my pinky out to her.

"Consider this a solemn vow, then." She links her pinky with mine and we both kiss our thumbs. "I'll never let my slight acrophobia keep you from greatness."

She huffs out a laugh, and we bring our hands down to swing between us. Imani is a little brighter after that, and as we stand in line at the booth, she talks more than she has since we got to Farmland. And, because I am a love scientist, it's about Peter!

"I just think he's funny. Guys usually think you're supposed to laugh at anything they say just because the patriarchy is insidious even on a micro level." A corner of her mouth ticks up and I know then that I've done it. My magnum opus is finding Imani a beau at Farmland. God, I deserve a Pulitzer. Or a Nobel. I can't remember the difference, but either one will do. "He really works for it, you know? He tries to earn every smile. It's . . . nice."

We're next in line for tickets, and I'm already planning their wedding and deciding what I want their kids to call me—Auntie Liv? Titi Livi?

She rolls her eyes at herself. "But who cares about all that when we're finally about to ride this thing? You weren't the only one checking the message boards, you know. This is like some music festival behemoth."

"What's bigger than behemoth? Colossal? Because if so, it's that," I add. She laughs her low, rich laugh that reminds me of only the best things.

The attendant at the booth is holding her hand out for our ticket money when both of our phones buzz. The next clue for the scavenger hunt appears—the only things visible in the picture are a checkered background and the apple in the foreground—and because we can't take any chances of not getting the next apple before someone else takes it, I start back in the direction of where we left Toni and Peter.

"Olivia, wait!" Imani calls from behind me. I don't know why she's still standing in line when she got the same notification that I did, but her feet are planted when I turn back. I know she's excited to ride this thing, but we have two more days, and we need to get this apple *now*. She twists her ring absently. "We can't just do this really fast?"

"We'll ride it later, I promise! But we're losing precious time, Mani—this is an emergency." I feel my entire body start to vibrate. This is it. This is what we came here for: an adventure. A big weekend. Everything can be good if we let it.

I smile wide and start power-walking. It takes a few seconds, but I finally hear Imani's footsteps behind me, and I give myself over to the thrill of this new kind of chase.

≋TONI≋

FRIDAY AFTERNOON

When Olivia and Imani come back after we get the next apple clue alert, Olivia sweeps in like a flash, her eyes bright and excited. My heart pounds a little at the sight, and I can't tell if it's in anticipation or fear. The fact that I don't know somehow makes it even more intense.

"You know where this is, right?" Olivia points at her phone screen. She's breathing hard from her walk over but looks energized instead of exhausted. Imani, on the other hand, just looks fed up.

She sweeps her long hair over her shoulder and stares straight ahead. It's almost like the rest of us aren't here, standing in a circle examining the clue on our respective phones. The look reminds me too much of myself—or the myself I am when I'm doing whatever this is with this girl I just met—to be comfortable. I look back down at my phone and focus on the task at hand.

"See that black-and-white checkered wall blurred in the background?" It's barely there and impossible to see if you're not looking for it, but I know these grounds like the back of my hand. There's only one place it could be.

We weave through the Core, and Peter winks at me over Imani's head and raises his eyebrows in silent code: *Dude, look! We're on a double date!* I can see it in his eyes; he's going to go all crush-stupid over this girl he barely knows, despite my years of advice to the contrary. He didn't say it explicitly while Olivia and Imani left for the Ferris wheel and the two of us stayed for the next set, but he might as well have. Peter is just like that—almost obsessive in his passions.

I bring us to a stop in front of the metal-roofed, glass-walled structure near the back of the Core. I hold my hand out in the most lackluster *ta da!* motion I can manage, even though I'm proud to have cracked another mystery. Olivia smirks, like she knows more than she's letting on about how I feel but she doesn't mention it.

"Silent Disco?" she asks, eyebrows raised. "You really think it's in there?"

I look around her body and examine the scene. The Silent Disco pavilion is filled with people wearing huge headphones and dancing to whatever is playing through them. It seems like a horror movie to me, but Olivia looks thrilled at this development.

I nod. "Behind the old DJ booth."

I try not to get caught up in my memory of seeing the back of the DJ booth for the first time—too young to see over the turntable as my dad spoke to his old friend. Back before it was the newly remodeled Silent Disco at all, and it was just the Disco—a retro-inspired all-day, all-ages dance party, and one of my dad's favorite activities to take me to as a kid. It felt like he knew everyone, and everything, back then.

"You have to crawl behind the booth to get to it. But the paneling down there is covered in checkered wallpaper." I rub the back of my neck and explain, "This whole place used to be a mashup of different decades. Checkered patterns for the fifties. Disco ball for the seventies. Neon colors everywhere for the eighties."

"I love it when you pull out your endless well of knowledge, Toni Baloney. Let's do this!" Peter rubs his hands together and volunteers to go inside. He looks at Imani, waiting for her to make a move toward the pavilion, and his expression is so open and hopeful. I feel the warm flash of annoyance light quick and indignant up my spine on my best friend's behalf when she crosses her arms over her chest and dismissively answers, "I'd rather not."

Peter, eternally undeterred, bounces on the balls of his feet anyway. He and Olivia take off to get in line and head in, and me and Imani are left standing side by side. We're surrounded by the ambient noise of laughter and music playing, but there's an obvious silence between the two of us as we wait.

"Are you afraid of heights?" she asks after a few minutes. She doesn't look at me.

"No," I respond slowly. I don't know if this is a test, but if it is, I'm sure I'm failing. "Are you?"

She presses her lips together and turns away without answering. I wonder what I could have done wrong to this girl to make her hate me so much so quickly, but Peter and Olivia bound out of the pavilion and pull my attention away. Peter is clutching the golden apple in both hands like he's afraid of dropping it, and Olivia has her arms spread wide like she's the master of the universe.

"We all gotta go back in there together!" Peter says once he reaches us. "Imani, I think you would like it. I have it on good authority that at least one of the headphones is playing Pop Top."

Imani doesn't look thrilled by the idea, but Olivia's face lights up. She snaps her fingers like she's just solved a great mystery.

"You two should go!" She points at the two of them. "Me and Toni need to practice for tomorrow, and I think we're probably out of clues for a while."

She looks at me for backup, raising her eyebrows like I should agree. But Peter cuts in first.

"Yeah, we can go dance and these two can go rehearse! I, for one, am tone deaf, so I'm pretty sure I'd be more of a hindrance than a help. What do you say, Imani?" Peter looks at her expectantly, but she looks at Olivia instead. They seem to communicate exclusively using a series of elaborate blinks.

Finally, Imani sighs. "Sure. Okay, let's go."

Peter practically skips back to the Silent Disco pavilion, a reluctant Imani dragging her feet behind him. I look at Olivia, where she charges ahead of me, the hem of her dress swaying when she walks like even her steps are a dance. I glance back at Peter, cheesing at Imani in line. I wonder how any of us ended up here. I wonder if it even matters.

OLIVIA

FRIDAY EVENING

We have to head back to camp since that's where Toni's guitar is, and I'm feeling like Ginger Rogers or, like, Fred Astaire or something. Like I'm walking on air. Everything is coming together perfectly. Imani and Peter are well on their way to hitting it off with just a few more nudges in the right direction, we're finding all the apples, and Toni's face looks marginally less murderous than it did this morning. All we have to do is rehearse, and barring me screwing things up somehow, we could even make a decent showing at the competition tomorrow.

And because I'm feeling so great, of course that's when I choose to check my phone.

A few notifications have popped up in the time it took to find the last apple. There are the usuals: a few texts from my mom asking how Bible camp is. I send her a quick response with a Googled scripture and try to ignore the pang of guilt.

It's not like I'm being missed, I remind myself with a snort. She's probably just wondering why her blood pressure has returned to normal levels for the first time since I was old enough to talk.

When I close my texts and open up my Confidential app, I brace myself. There are a couple Confidential DMs from a burner account with no profile picture, and my stomach drops immediately. I've been getting these every day since last semester, despite locking my account months ago, and they still manage to make me feel sick to my stomach every time.

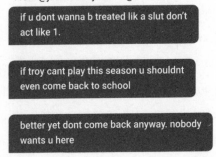

From @justice4troy000 to @OliviaTwist:

> if u dont wanna b treated lik a slut don't act like 1.

> if troy cant play this season u shouldnt even come back to school

> better yet dont come back anyway. nobody wants u here

I delete the messages quickly and don't even bother reporting the account. It doesn't matter anyway, I know, because a new one will just pop up in its place tomorrow. As it turns out, the people at my school who take pride in harassing me online have an endless pool of email addresses to pull from. And Confidential—a site started by local high school students as a *Big Brother*-esque social site meant almost exclusively to share gossip—well, clearly their priorities are not on the side of shutting down trolls. I turn off my push notifications so at least tomorrow this won't be the first thing I see.

I'm suddenly tired. I'm so tired of all of this. I don't want to go back to school in a week. I don't want any of it. I just want to go back to first semester, before Troy Murphy had ever paid me any attention. This is miles away from how I imagined my senior year. But I hope against hope that things can go back to normal. All it's going to take is my silence.

As we walk, my mind begins the spiral it always does whenever I accidentally think about what's coming next week. If you're like me, after the breakup to end all breakups, you may never recover. Your life might never be the same.

Not because you loved them so much or because you thought they were the one, but because you thought that you—stripped down to your barest parts—might actually be good enough to hold on to them. That someone like Troy Murphy could ever really love a girl like me.

The type of girl who feels too much and talks too much and does all the wrong things at the wrong times.

"Olivia. You okay?" Toni asks.

I look up from my phone and realize I've stopped in the middle of a pathway and people are stepping to the side to avoid running into me. We're outside the Core, back on the makeshift gravel streets that lead back to the campsites.

My stomach clenches. My eyes start to burn a little like I'm getting ready to cry. So I do what I do best. I decide to change course. I need something else, something far away from goals and tasks and that look in Toni's eye right now that's dangerously close to pity. I don't want to be pitied. I don't want to feel anything at all like what I'm feeling right now.

I'm itching for the sensation of getting lost in a crowd, absorbed by sound and bodies and movement. The way becoming part of that sweaty, strange mass has always managed to soothe that noise in the back of my mind, constantly buzzing with the refrain of *too much too much too much*.

And a part of me, a bigger part than I should admit, is hoping Toni gets it. I grab her hand to lead her back toward the Core and spare a second just long enough to pray that she won't pull away. I don't know what I'll do in this moment if she does.

I look back at her, her eyebrows raised high, skin shining with the same thin layer of sweat I can sense on my own face. I hope that my gut is right about her.

I hope she's ready to get free.

TONI

FRIDAY EVENING

"I don't know about this."

Her back is to the massive barn in front of us, but everything about her stance indicates that all she wants to do is turn around and run straight inside. In all my years of attending Farmland, I've never been in any of the dance barns before—huge wooden structures that used to house horses and hay bales when this was a functioning farm but have supposedly been changed into pretty impressive imitations of clubs—but it looms large in front of us against the near-darkness of the evening sky.

"What's wrong? Is EDM not your thing? I think there's probably a barn that has, like, pop maybe? Or folk?" she asks. She's close to me, but I still have to strain to hear her over the sound of the bass coming from the barn.

I take my hat off and run a hand through my locs before putting it back on. I don't want to go into the giant barn in front of us. This is the one area of Farmland I've never dared venture to before because I don't, under any circumstances, dance. I have a lot of rules that govern the way I move through the world, but this is at the top of my DON'T list in blinking neon letters.

My rational brain knows that we should go back to camp, knows that we have to rehearse together before tomorrow, knows that if I want to have any shot of winning the Golden Apple and getting closer to that moment of enlightenment on stage that my dad always recollected, then I have no choice. But my lesser self isn't there yet.

It's embarrassing to admit, even in just my own head, but I'm scared.

But also, the thought of playing my guitar in front of anybody, but especially Olivia, makes my heart beat faster than is strictly healthy. I'm scared to pick up my guitar again and not be as good as I once was, I'm scared that even if the skill comes back, nothing else will. I'm terrified that the passion, the contentedness, the connection that I used to have to the music might be gone for good. And that's enough of a reason to get me to consider that even though Olivia won't say why she wants to bail on rehearsing for now, maybe going inside this massive nightmarebarn is worth it to get me out of having to admit that I don't know if I can do this at all.

"No, it's not . . . It's not the genre. It's just that. I don't. You know. *Dance.*" I try to sound less embarrassed about it than I am but I know I'm not successful when Olivia's eyes sparkle a little and she cocks her head to the side.

"What do you mean you don't dance?"

It's so stupid being embarrassed about something like this, something I've never been embarrassed about before, but I am. It's just that Olivia is looking up at me with those big brown eyes of hers and she is fearless, the type of person who just throws themselves into something and believes the best. And here I am, too scared to be honest about why I don't want to play my guitar in front of her, but also too scared to buy myself some time by dancing in front of some people I'll never see again.

Her face softens and she puts a hand on my shoulder. And it's almost alarming how fast my defenses come tumbling down. Something about the tenderness of the gesture makes me want to be honest.

"I just don't. And with good reason." I put my hand on my forehead and groan. Here it is, the moment of truth. Time to shatter the illusion of being self-contained and unaffected. "This is so humiliating. Just forget I said anything. Let's dance." I try to side-step her and head inside, but she's too quick. She moves in front of me and puts her hands on her hips.

"Nuh-uh. Me and you have a deal going here, Toni. A partnership, if you will. And I've been told that no partnership works if it's not honest."

She looks so serious and stern with her finger wagging at me, it's enough to make me laugh, just a little. "And who told you that?"

"*Teen Vogue*, obviously. Right after they taught me how to dismantle the patriarchy." She smirks. "Now please continue."

"You can't make fun of me."

"I would never!"

"The fact that that's a lie is written all over your face."

She makes a motion like she's zipping her lips, and I roll my eyes. It feels like before, back when we were sitting in the grass during the Pop Top show. There's an ease that settles in me when I talk to her, the ability to resist sharing dissolving into thin air without my permission.

"Okay so the only party I ever went to, I . . . well, what you need to know is that it's hard for someone with arms like mine to really *move*, you know, without committing acts of dance-induced homicide. Anyway I was pretty much alone on the makeshift dance floor in this girl's basement until this girl tapped me on my shoulder to ask me to dance."

"Oh no," Olivia says, because she must know where this is headed.

"Oh yes," I say. "I was shocked, and had definitely just caught a secondhand high from some people in the corner, so when I turned around I didn't know how close her face was to my elbow and—"

"You broke her nose, didn't you?" Her eyes go wide and her voice adds in a whisper, "Oh, Toni, you precious baby gazelle."

I don't even have to answer, because the well of self-restraint that Olivia has been holding in seems to burst at once and she's giggling uncontrollably. And I don't know what it is about the way it happens, the way her face looks more than a little sympathetic but also deeply amused, but it makes me want to laugh too. One of those deep, honest laughs that you can't really help but feel in your bones. I can't remember the last time I laughed like this, and I don't even think anything is that funny.

It's just something about her, standing in front of me, happy and light, that makes her energy infectious. I don't know why she even wants to dance with me, why she doesn't dip out to do her own thing between clues. It's not like I'm a lot of fun, really. I mean, Peter thinks I'm funny, but that's because he's the only straight man on the face of the earth that I think isn't worth tossing out aside from Paul Rudd and LeVar Burton. But people like Olivia aren't normally drawn to people like me.

We finally reach the front of the line, and the volunteer at the door holds out her hand for Olivia's wrist. When she stamps her and waves her in, Olivia adds, "I swear to protect my nose. You don't have to worry about me." She holds her hand up in an incorrect boy scout salute, grinning. "And I vow to hold your secret with me as long as we both shall live."

I sigh once and stick my arm out to be stamped as well.

"You better watch your face. I'm not kidding about being a menace to society." I think she might say something in response, but the moment the doors open and we step in, I can't hear anything else but the pulsing sound of the bass.

The barn looks surprisingly club-like, despite the dirt floor and the lofted beams that still hold hay bales as if an animal could trot in here at any time, looking to graze. There are about a hundred people in the barn, dancing to whatever it is the DJ is currently playing. They're moving together, some with more rhythm than others, but everyone seems wholly unconcerned with what anyone else thinks. I don't want to move, but that seems out of the question as Olivia grabs my wrist and pulls us to the center of the dance floor.

There is a disco ball above us that casts prisms of light across her face as she turns it to the ceiling. We're close, but not close enough to touch. The back of my brain is screaming *retreat!* but I can't bring myself to listen to it. All I want to do is watch Olivia move as she allows the music to take her. It's *everything*.

When she opens her eyes and sees me staring, I don't look away even though I want to. I want to be honest, like she said. And my most honest self just wants to watch her get lost in this right now, whether I know how to dance or not.

But she doesn't let me get away with it that easy.

She reaches for me, softly wrapping her fingers around my wrists and tugging me closer. It's so slow and gentle it's completely at odds with the way people are moving around us, the mass of bodies pulsing and crashing together like atoms. But in the center of all the chaos it's just me and Olivia, my hands barely grazing her hips as she sways. She smiles and my heart feels like it's in my throat. I'm not sure what to do, how to catalog this sensation.

Only one person has ever let me down, because I've refused to care enough about any of the people who've come into my life to give them that much power. I've backed myself into a corner, watched the people around me group up and pair off, and until I met Olivia, I hadn't realized just how lonely that existence had been. Sure, I'd had fleeting thoughts of what a relationship might be like before, but those thoughts had never been enough for me to want to pursue one—for me to take the chance at what it would feel like when that relationship failed.

I'm a runner. My dad was a runner. He never learned how to stand in a feeling for long enough to pick it apart. But all Dad's running ever did was carry him further and further away from the people who loved him the most. All it gave him was a restless heart and a daughter who only knew him through stolen moments between tours, anecdotes of life on the road, and guitar riffs.

Maybe that was enough for him. And maybe, for a long time, I could convince myself that it was enough for me. But not anymore. Not right now.

Here, in this moment, I'm anchored. I'm facing this girl and the bigness of this head-on.

Trust me, she mouths. My palms are sweating. I've only ever trusted three people in my life—never gotten close enough to trust any more. I hold on to her waist a little tighter.

And I answer with my body: *I do.*

OLIVIA

FRIDAY NIGHT

Even if Toni doesn't feel comfortable out here, dancing is something I know. The dance floor is my territory, the one place I feel completely in control of my own body and totally myself. Imani always says it's like flipping a switch, watching me go from the Olivia who acts like what other people want me to be and becoming the Olivia who is wholly her own, who moves with grace, barely contained energy, perfectly in time with the music.

I start to move. I hope that Toni will just catch on as I go. I close my eyes and breathe deeply. The room smells like sweat and earthy red clay that people have trailed in from outside, but I can't even hate it. There are bodies pressing in from every side, but it's not suffocating, it's liberating. In this moment, all of us are moving together, one sweaty mass finding comfort in the same thing. I bring my arms over my head and allow the rhythm to take over.

One song switches to another, and then another and another and my eyes are still closed. A body brushes against mine from the side, and all of a sudden, I'm taken back to another party. I'm not in the dance barn anymore, I'm in someone's house. The music isn't EDM, it's some trap song I've never heard before, and the body against my back isn't a stranger. It's the same person who told me they would say they loved me back if I just stopped *being such a nun about everything.*

"If you cared about me, you would," he muttered in my ear, breath hot. He could've been talking about anything, really. The pictures he wanted but I was afraid to send, the fact that we'd been dating for three weeks and hadn't done anything more than make out in the back seat of his precious Charger, even though he wanted to. My mouth suddenly feels like there's sawdust in it.

My eyes blink open quickly, and there's no Troy Murphy in front of me with a red Solo cup and his stupid Park Meade High School Varsity Basketball letter jacket that I used to think was so special. That I used to feel so valued in when he'd drape it over my shoulders in the hallway. There's just Toni, and my heart slows at the sight. Toni is safe. Me and Toni have a deal, an even trade. A smile is just a smile and a jacket is just a jacket.

Her eyes are closed now too, and she's moving with her arms

still pretty firmly locked to my waist but moving nonetheless. She's swaying with the beat, allowing herself to get lost in it.

When she opens her eyes, I don't pretend I wasn't staring. And I don't expect the look I see on her face, all hopeful and open. It's different than the half-scowl she's been sporting practically since the moment we met, but it's perfect on her face. It makes her look younger, like the type of person who eats ice cream even though it's cold outside and wears white after Labor Day because what are rules?

If I had met Toni in a different life, was born a different person with a different personality and absolutely no baggage to carry from a million failed not-quite-love stories, then I would think she is the type of girl you write home about. I mean, not *write* write, because no one is Jo March-ing it like that anymore, but you know. The type of girl you tell your parents you're bringing home for the holidays.

She's beautiful. I try to ignore how that beauty is making me feel, but the part of my brain that never quite shuts off convinces me it's safe to think. Under these lights, skin dark and luminous and shining, it's okay for me to admire her. But she was beautiful when she was leaning against the performance barn earlier clearly freaking out, and when she was sprawled in the dirt after tripping that girl in those fairy wings, and as she was explaining what it means for a vocalist to hit an A above high C while we were walking by a set earlier too.

And . . . there it is. I don't know how I was able to ignore it earlier. Of course I'm developing a crush on her. I can see Imani's disappointed face already. I can see my mom with her head in her hands, looking tired and sitting at the kitchen table after she found out what happened with me and Troy, saying, "Why can't you be more like your sister, Olivia? Why can't you slow down?"

The song changes, and Toni isn't smiling anymore. She just looks at me, but not like people on the other end of the *Olivia loves [insert name here]* equation usually do. She's looking at me like she sees me. And then she's moving gradually closer, eyes still open, and I could do it. My body and my brain are in a battle to the death to just let this happen, to give myself over to this good moment and this great feeling and to Toni. And maybe it wouldn't be so bad, I think, letting myself. It's as natural to me as riding a bike, the moment of breathlessness just before a big kiss. Her hands twitch just slightly on my waist, I lean in, flick my eyes up just before shutting them and—

I stop short. Something catches my eye on the loft just over her shoulder, something gold and glittering nestled on top of one of the big bundles of hay. The next apple. It's enough to snap me out of it, and I practically jump back when I realize.

I almost ruined everything. I almost let my stupid instincts drive me into another poorly timed romance that would end in ruin. All before I was able to help Toni win the competition, perfect my wing-woman game to get Imani and Peter together, and of course, win the scavenger hunt. The golden apple is a sign. My mom would call it divine intervention. But I'm just going to call it fate finally throwing me a bone and saving me from my own recklessness for once.

I step back and point behind her. I shake myself a little, and take a deep breath. I've killed the moment, and probably reversed whatever ground we'd managed to cover since earlier today when she would barely speak to me. But she just blinks, like she's coming back to her senses, and my stomach clenches a little. Because *that's* the look that I should expect to see. *A brief moment of insanity is all that was*, I think.

She follows my finger to the apple against the back wall. We haven't gotten the clue yet, but we didn't need to. I try on a smile that feels more like a dog baring its teeth than a girl trying to pretend everything is normal, and step around her to go grab it.

I try to tell myself it doesn't sting just a little bit. I wanted to forget, and for a while I did. For a second as she was holding me, and the music was moving us, I was only thinking about her. This moment. This place.

That's all I wanted from this weekend anyway.

Right?

TONI

FRIDAY NIGHT

Quid pro quo. My cart, your wagon.

She told me. We agreed. I mean, it's not like she didn't at least give me some kind of warning that the direction I was heading I was heading by myself. I don't know what came over me. I don't know why I thought dancing together meant more than just dancing together. I swallow down the bitter taste of embarrassment and try to smile as she walks back with the fourth apple.

She had room in her fanny pack for it since she handed the rest to Peter earlier, so she zips it up and nods at the door. By the time we emerge, it's dark in the way that it only ever gets dark at Farmland. The illusion of stars created by the lights from the stages and the carnival rides in the Core making a hazy sky, half blackened, half sparkling.

Olivia yawns next to me and I try to ignore the way her shoulder bumps mine every few steps like she's too tired to hold herself up.

"Not bad for your first time at the rodeo," Olivia says, jerking her thumb over her shoulder at the barn. She smiles sleepily up at me. I think it's a little early for her to be yawning, but then I remember the toll being at a festival can take on your body the first time. Twelve hours in the hot sun, walking miles and miles, and standing or dancing in between those times can wear on a person. "You didn't impale anyone even a little bit. I knew you had it in you."

I smile, but I don't speak. Not because I'm afraid of saying something that lets her get too close to me or, because that ship has well and truly sailed, but because there's something about this moment that I don't want to change with words.

The fact is, I like hanging out with Olivia. I like it when she calls me out and when she pushes me to dance in dirty barns and when she says a little more than she probably should. We had a deal, and tomorrow after the competition and after we find the last apple, we'll probably never see each other again. I'm going to hold up my end of the bargain, and she's going to hold up hers, and that's how we're going to handle this.

"You have a lot of confidence in me for someone who just met me today," I answer.

She stretches and yawns again but doesn't respond. I'm coming down from the buzz of the dance party and am feeling some of the adrenaline drain out of me too. I'm more practiced at staying up late and braving the exhaustion that comes along with the heat than she is though, so I do a better job at powering through.

"Well, Toni," she says between another yawn. "I have a way of knowing these things."

Once we get back to the area with our tents, Olivia turns toward my campsite without hesitation. I almost speak up to stop her, and then I remember. Of course, we still need to rehearse. A nervous energy courses through me. I reach into my pocket and run my thumb over the cheap plastic pick I keep on me at all times to distract myself from the feeling.

We walk past a couple that's around my mom's age, who must've set up camp after we left for the Core this morning, right across from ours. They tilt their cans of White Claw toward us in greeting and smile at us as we pass. I can tell by their full setup they've done this before: tent, Farmland flag with the three-apple logo in the center, canopy tent, gazebo, tapestries hung up around the canopy to shield it from the sun. I have to fight the urge to salute them. I have a certain reverence for Farmland veterans.

Olivia falls into the frayed foldable camping chair that I set up outside my tent and lets her head fall back to look at the sky.

"Can you believe that we get to be here? This is some next-level cosmic intervention."

I sit on the small cooler that holds the already-melted ice and a bunch of bottled water and bananas. I stretch my legs out in front of me and look up too.

"Do you believe in signs?" Olivia whispers.

"What do you mean?"

"I mean"—she waves her hand around everything near us—"do you believe that everything happens for a reason? That you stopping to help me and my breathing going haywire and your competition and my scavenger hunt practically forcing us together is a sign?"

"I guess that depends," I say, plucking a blade of grass from beside me and twisting it around my index finger. "A sign of what?"

I can see her answer forming, no doubt something a little woo-woo and over my head, before her eye catches on the window of the truck. I know immediately what she's spotted before she says anything.

"Your guitar!" She sits up, suddenly wide awake. When she points at me, I wince at what I'm sure is the next question: *If you're so serious about this, shouldn't we start practicing now?* "You know the lead singer from Sonny Blue didn't pick up a guitar until she was thirty? 'The Argonauts' was the first song she ever wrote."

I freeze. "What?"

I couldn't have heard her correctly.

"Yeah, it's completely amazing. I've listened to, like, eight hundred interviews of hers. She talks about it sometimes—how she couldn't afford a guitar or lessons growing up, so she didn't even buy one until she was way older. How cool is that? Finding your passion at thirty instead of eighteen?" She sighs. "It's like everyone is supposed to know everything before they've even left high school, you know? Bonnie is proof that rushing is overrated."

"I . . . Yeah. That is amazing."

There's something refreshing about hearing her give voice to what I've been thinking since before the summer started—that I'm not sure about much of anything anymore.

"They, um, had this demo that never made it to an album that I really like. It's called 'Too Much, Too Soon,'" I say. I clear my throat a little, unsure why I'm sharing but not stopping. "My dad used to love this song. He taught me to play it."

I reach into the truck and grab my case. I take my guitar out and I play the opening notes for her, and for once, thinking about my dad doesn't make my throat constrict with the telltale sign of incoming tears. In this memory, I'm thirteen and sitting in the basement with my first acoustic in my lap. He's just finished working on Sonny Blue's first summer tour—the one where they opened for Mumford & Sons.

"Try this." He reaches over and changes the way my fingers are arranged on the strings. He smiles when I get it and I'm able to switch easily between one chord and the next. "There you go, TJ. You are gonna be *big* one day, you know that?"

I roll my eyes, because I'm thirteen and rolling my eyes is law, and because Dad knows that will never happen. I'll never play outside this basement, and I'll never tell anyone that I play at all. This music thing lives and dies right here.

"I'm not going to be famous, Dad."

"I didn't say *famous*, kid, I said you were going to be big! There's a difference." He strums a little and I follow his lead. He closes his eyes and nods his head along with the music. "You don't need an audience to be big. Don't forget that."

He opens his eyes and slaps a hand against his thigh as I continue strumming.

"Why you moving so fast, little girl? Who told you you couldn't have the whole world?" he sings quietly. His voice is just as heartstoppingly beautiful as always.

In these moments, I know my voice probably won't ever be able to do what his can—wrapping around everything in a space until it's the only thing you can feel—but I can make up for it with my skill on guitar.

The time I spend playing with him are stolen moments before he's back on tour, but I take them so seriously. I work so hard. I learn so quickly. I try to make him proud of me.

"Whoa," I say when he finishes. "What is that?"

"A song I heard from that band I was with this summer. Sonny Blue?"

He looks up suddenly and I know he can hear my mom's keys in the lock just like I can. My heart sinks. When she comes in, we'll stop, he'll go upstairs to greet her, and they'll either be sickeningly sweet for the rest of the night or I'll have to resign myself to my room and slide my noise-canceling headphones on to avoid listening to them fight.

There are only ever two options, and something tells me tonight is going to be the latter.

He looks back at me with a smile that is as wide as it is fake. He puts his guitar back on the stand and takes mine to hang it up on the wall. It's incredible how quickly everything in the room shifts back to normal. To empty.

"When I say big, you know that feeling you just got? That's what I mean." He jerks his head in the direction of the stairs. "Let's go help your mom with the groceries."

Why you moving so fast, little girl? Who told you you couldn't have the whole world?

I swallow as Olivia looks at me without expectation, but with clear excitement. I'm a little rusty now, I know. I haven't played in practically a year, but as I finish the last verse, my singing voice hoarse with disuse, I feel not good exactly, but relieved. Playing that song is like breaking through the surface of a pool after being underwater for too long. It feels like coming home.

"Well, it's a good thing Sonny Blue never released that song," she says when I set the guitar back into my dad's case. My heart stops beating for a second. It doesn't sound like she means it to be an insult, not with the way she's smiling at me, but I can't help but take it as one.

"Why not?"

"Because"—she nudges her sandal against my boot—"it would've been pretty embarrassing for Bonnie Harrison to have been outsung and outplayed so thoroughly by one of her fans." She smiles and my entire body relaxes. "I mean it. A cover that's better than the original? The power that that has? Unmatched."

My face gets warm, and I'm grateful for both the cover of darkness and my skin tone for hiding what would almost certainly be a blush on a lighter-skinned person.

"You've never even heard the original."

She holds her hand over her heart and gasps. "I'm offended by your lack of faith in my judgment!" She winces as she adds a brief amendment. "Which, okay, I will admit is occasionally questionable, but in this case is absolutely trustworthy."

"Trustworthy, huh?" I ask.

"Absolutely unimpeachable." She holds my gaze for a moment longer than I know what to do with and my skin feels like it's vibrating. I stand up and stretch even though I don't really need to. I just have to find something to do with my hands.

"Is this what you want to do now that you're out in the big, bad world?" She studies me and crosses her legs at her ankles. "Become a massive rock star?"

"I'm supposed to start college next week." I shrug. "Maybe grad school eventually, law school like my mom. I don't know."

It feels like a lie, sort of, as I say it. Somehow, the feeling of playing that song for her just a few moments ago vibrates through me. It felt so right, so unlike it has at any other point in the past eight months. I practically have to scold myself for even thinking it. Just because it feels good doesn't make it a plan. I'm performing here to come up with a plan, to have some Truth about my life revealed to me like my dad always promised would happen.

Besides, even if it were more than just a whim, I couldn't pursue music without breaking my mom's heart anyway. It's the definition of a nonstarter.

Olivia doesn't respond right away, she just nods her head and taps her lips like she's thinking. It's silent between us, but the nighttime chorus of festival noise rages on: the muted bands playing in the distance, the shouts of laughter coming from a couple campsites away, a car crunching over gravel. It's one of my favorite songs.

"You know what to do," she says, after a while. I almost forgot we were in the middle of a conversation. "Even if you don't know that you know, it's in there somewhere."

"You think?" I ask. I lean back in my chair, trying to be cool. I do what I did all through high school: I paint an expression on my face that reads ambivalent, above it all, disaffected. But when Olivia stares at me for a second, I know my usual go-to is falling short. She's seeing me, the Toni that I used to save for when my dad had taken off on another tour and my mom was holed up in her room, pretending not to be heartbroken: young, vulnerable, lonelier than she cares to admit.

"Yeah." She nods. "I really do."

Her voice is sure. Not a hint of doubt in it. She's only known me for less than twelve hours, but in her estimation, that's enough time to know this. Like my dad, I'm beginning to realize Olivia has her Truths too.

She's a mess of contradictions. Equal parts confident and awkward. Just as likely to anxiously fidget with her hands or her clothes as she is to completely lose herself to a song she's never heard before.

"So that's the song you want to do tomorrow?" she asks, after it takes me too long to respond.

When I nod, she claps her hands together once. "Okay then. Let's practice."

I look around, like someone will hop out and say that's not a great idea. But of course, it's just me, sputtering, tendrils of nerves still hanging on. But Olivia has committed to helping me, and I'm committed to figuring my shit out. I grab my capo out of the hard case to play this in a key I think will be better suited for Olivia's register. She pulls her chair forward a bit so we're even closer together, offers to take the high parts, and we just . . . go.

It's cliché to say that our voices dance together seamlessly, or that her lilting soprano is the perfect complement to my alto, but whatever we do works. We're in it. She's offering suggestions—*I know what I'm talking about! I was in concert choir for two entire years before I got kicked out for an incident involving hair dye and half the tenor section at State. Don't ask*—and trusting my notes when I have them.

Two hours pass before Olivia's eyes start to look so heavy I'm afraid she's going to fall asleep in the middle of the bridge. When we finish the song, she stands, yawns, and stretches her arms over her head.

I want this to work, I realize. This feels like more than a last-ditch effort to figure my life out. I want to sing that song with her and I want to win and I want to believe that music still holds some answers for me. That the way I feel right now means something.

"So we're definitely doing this," I say. Until we started singing together, I guess a part of me still figured this was all going to be a fluke. That Olivia wouldn't be able to sing, that I'd freeze when it came time to finally play, that even if everything worked exactly right, the two of us just wouldn't click. But none of that happened.

Olivia simply nods, like she understands all that I'm not saying. It's nice, feeling like we're communicating without exchanging any words. I turn my face up to the sky to see what she's seeing, and try to ignore the way the warmth spreads through my chest.

Maybe I should tell her the truth about what happened to my dad. If she's going to do this with me, if we're going to be in this together, then she might need to know. But when I look at her, looking at the stars, I know that's not an option. She's happy and I—I feel as close to happy as I've been in months too. And I just can't. I know enough to know that some dark corners inside us are better left dark, and Olivia is all light.

"Oh my God. Oh my *God!*" she shrieks. I think she must have stepped on something again, so I leap into action, ready to patch up another festival injury. But when I crouch down next to her, Olivia is giggling and shaking her head in disbelief at the same time. "My best friend is in love!"

She holds up her phone and shows me a picture of Peter

drooling all over a sleeping bag in their tent, UNO cards stuck to his face, with a text underneath:

> I went to the bathroom for five minutes and came back to this 😬

I laugh at Peter's slack, drooling, sleep-of-the-innocent face.

"Imani is totally buying me a new one." She pouts. "I didn't even get a chance to sleep in it!"

"I don't know how he manages it, but the guy can fall asleep anywhere, under any conditions. And stay asleep despite every attempt to get him to wake up." I think about trying to get him up in time to catch his flight last time he came to town, and barely keep myself from shuddering. The memory of a frantic Peter, half-dressed and sleep-mussed, running through security at Indianapolis International Airport isn't a scene I'd like to repeat anytime soon. "I think you might have to consider your sleeping bag collateral damage in the Peter Menon Experience."

She doesn't respond right away, so I add, "You can, um, stay here. If you want. I have a pretty massive air mattress. You and Imani, I mean. We can just, um, trade tents for the night?"

I hate that my voice comes out sounding like a question, but I'm out of my depth here. I can't wrangle Peter back to our campsite, so maybe a switch is our best bet? I can't read her expression as she looks up at me. She cocks her head to the side like she's trying to figure me out, and after a few hour-long seconds, she nods once like she's figured everything out.

She quickly types something on her phone before responding, "I'll just stay. I'll have you know, if you're dangerous to dance with, then I'm lethal to share a bed with."

I'm practically operating on autopilot as I reach into my duffel bag and pull out a spare tank top and some old softball shorts. I'm going to share sleeping quarters with a living, breathing human being who also happens to be someone I thought I might kiss a few hours ago. I hand everything over to her, take a deep breath, and think, *This is going to be okay. Yes, we'll be sleeping not even two feet away from each other while she wears your clothes, but this is* fine.

I'm the cartoon dog in the fire meme in human form.

She clutches the clothes to her chest. She looks between me and the tent and then back at me again before mumbling, strangely shy, "You'll stay out here while I'm changing though, right?"

It seems like such a strange question, such a no-brainer—because why would I invade her privacy like that?—that my nod is slow. It seems to be enough for her though because suddenly she's smiling again. She kicks off her Birks and unzips the tent. She turns around once she gets inside, and pokes her head out of the flap.

"You're a good egg, Toni," she says. She zips it up behind her and I sit back down on the cooler.

This feeling is nothing like playing in front of her a few hours ago—this fear settles in my stomach and not my chest. It's strange and scary and warm. I can hear Olivia moving around inside, her elbows clumsily bumping into the nylon of the tent while she quietly sings the chorus of Kittredge's newest radio hit. She's so unguarded, it feels almost intimate.

My cheeks heat at the thought. And that's when I know this isn't fear at all. Not really. These are the butterflies Taylor Swift is talking about in all those songs I secretly love to play.

And there's no way I'm going to be able to shake them.

FARMLAND
MUSIC AND ARTS FESTIVAL
SATURDAY

"Hold your hands to the sky. [laughs] Yeah, I know it's raining. Now I want you to breathe. I want you to think about the person to your left and your right. Feel that? The boom boom, boom boom? [pauses] That's all of us. Hearts beating. Together. This next song is about that feeling. Keep your hands up. Sing along if you know the lyrics."

–Bonnie Harrison during Sonny Blue's first headline set at Farmland Music and Arts Festival, August 2015

OLIVIA

SATURDAY MORNING

The first thing I notice when I wake up is how warm I feel from where the sunlight is hitting my face, and I yawn without opening my eyes. I'm so cozy and secure nestled under my blanket, sprawled out all alone on my roomy mattress. But—I didn't bring a blanket to Farmland. I brought a sleeping bag. Oh my God. My eyes open instantly and I sit up, clutching the blanket to my chest, my heart practically in my throat. I shared a tent with Toni last night!

The realization hits me so fast and so hard I'm not sure how to even catalog how I feel. I mean . . . I shared a tent with Toni last night. It doesn't seem real as I keep thinking it, so I whisper it aloud to myself a couple of times, just to be sure.

"I shared a tent with Toni last night. Toni and I slept on the same mattress. Toni and me were in the same tent on the same mattress and—" I groan and run both hands down my face until I look like a Munch painting. "I didn't even wear my silk scarf to bed."

I barely get a chance to smooth my edges down and establish a game plan for emerging from this tent looking much more together than I feel before I'm being accosted by my beloved older sister. I swipe open her most recent text.

> I'm flying back to Boston today. Mom is driving me to the airport now.

It's been a long summer with Nia at home. Both she and Wash returned from Boston for the summer to internships at the same tech startup in downtown Indianapolis, her in their legal department and him in IT. Somehow they managed to make it through their freshman and sophomore years not only as the same Instagram-worthy couple, but also somehow even more . . . powerful.

Nia traded in her signature twenty-four-inch lace-front wigs for her natural hair, which is perfectly curly and never seems to get dry and brittle like mine (*You're not using the right products, Olivia, that's why. Haven't you done any research on natural hair maintenance?*), and her school uniform cardigans for statement T-shirts with sayings on them like DISMANTLE WHITE FEMINISM and NO HUMAN IS ILLEGAL ON STOLEN LAND.

She seemed more grounded and even surer of her convictions (*You're ordering camping gear from Amazon? Why don't you just punch a factory worker directly in the face next time? It would probably be less of a betrayal.*). Which meant, of course, that Mom is now even surer of her choice of the favorite daughter.

With Imani gone at her summer program, no one from school speaking to me anymore, and no car to drive aimlessly around town like every other bored kid I knew, there'd been nothing but time for both my mom and Nia to remind me what a disappointment I am. Conversations about me eventually choosing a major filled with insults about how I'd actually be chasing an MRS degree. Dinnertime arguments about me retaking my SATs or signing up for another AP test study group. Or worst of all, Nia's constant side-eyes that said more than any snippy comment ever could: *You've embarrassed this family once again, and this time there's no achievement of mine big enough to distract from it.*

I hated to admit it—because no one is supposed to think this about their sister—but by a week in, I was more than ready for her to go.

> Okay! Safe travels! Have a good semester!

Her response buzzes back almost instantly:

> How is it that can I hear you screaming even through texts? Jesus. Don't answer that.

> Make better choices this year.

I don't respond. I decide to delete the entire conversation for good measure. I just can't go there right now.

I wish I could say it wasn't always like this between me and Nia, but I've been the sideshow to her main attraction for a long time. Since Mom got her job as the college counselor at Park Meade, and Nia got the partial tuition break that comes along with it at the beginning of her freshman year, she became someone untouchable. And I became the embarrassing little sister that she wanted to escape. She had a new, picture-perfect, private school life at Park Meade. She could rub elbows with rich kids and talk a future in the Ivy Leagues, and I didn't fit into that.

I was a reminder of her life before—imperfect, nearly impossible to fix—and she's never let me forget it.

From our grades to the way we look—her model-long legs and narrow hips like my mom, and me with my curves for days and height that's entirely dependent on my collection of platform sandals—we've just never been on the same side of whatever line divides people who have it all together and the people who don't.

I lock my phone and try my best to settle the creeping insecurity that always comes after an interaction with my sister. I shake out my hands and roll my shoulders a few times, trying to get back to that feeling I had when I first woke up, instead of this aching feeling settling heavily over my body. Today is going to be a good day. I am going to help Toni with this competition. I am going to work my magic and make sure that Imani and Peter finally stop dancing around each other.

Even if it's just for this weekend, in these small ways, I can bring something good to the lives of people I care about. I rub my eyes just in case there's still sleep in them and crawl out of the tent, all disheveled and no-doubt gross looking.

Toni is sitting in one of the foldable camping chairs with her guitar in her lap, and last night comes rushing back to me. The sound of her voice, low and scratchy and perfect, perfectly complementing the sound of her gentle strumming. The way she sang a song that, even though I'd never heard it before, made it sound like greeting an old friend after too long away. I kind of wanted to sink into it. I kind of definitely want to hug her.

"Good morning," she says, looking up briefly through her thick eyelashes. I don't even try to think about what mine must look like right now, all caked together from not wiping off my makeup properly before going to sleep. It's skincare maintenance 101.

"What are you doing up? It's early." She holds out a banana to me in offering and I shake my head. "We pretty much just went to sleep a few hours ago."

The camps around us are still quiet and still but the muffled sound of distant soundchecks in the Core rings all the way to us.

"What can I say? Late to bed, early to rise makes a girl cranky, sassy, and snide. That's how that goes, right?" She huffs a laugh in response before turning her attention back to her guitar. She looks so comfortable with her acoustic in her hands and still a little sleepy. Her locs fall forward and frame her face as she tunes it silently while I just stand there, staring like an idiot.

My chest tightens momentarily. I should definitely leave. I should go back to my tent before I do something or say something that's going to mess this up. Things between us are going so well, I want to keep them that way, and my track record tells me the best way to do that is to make myself scarce. I don't want to leave her though. I don't want to walk away, even if it's just until the performance later.

I swallow down a lump in my throat and plaster on a smile.

"Our name is going to be in lights tonight!"

I clap my hands together and try to think happy, pleasant thoughts. But we're so close to the moment of truth, it's only a matter of time before I do what I always do. Maybe I'll accidentally step on the neck of Toni's guitar and break it before we even make it to the performance barn. Maybe I'll buy her a burrito at the taco cart that gives her food poisoning—oh God, what if *I* get food poisoning and she doesn't have a partner? You know what? I decide right then and there I won't eat until after we're done performing. And I'll go back to camp and grab my slippers, just in case. It never hurts to tread lightly.

We're one of the first slots after the lunch break ends, so we have a few hours to practice, see some shows, and maybe find another apple if a clue drops between now and then. But first, I need to pull myself together. I'm feeling jittery and unsure, and it always helps me to put on a cute dress and spend some time putting my makeup on. It's like donning a suit of armor. And with Nia's texts still floating around in my head, and my nerves about the performance later, I need all the help I can get.

"I know a creative genius like yourself must need some time alone to get into the right headspace, so I'm just going to grab my stuff and be out of your hair." I duck back into the tent to grab my clothes from the day before and say loud enough to be heard outside, "Just one second and I'll be ready to go!"

When I find my left sandal, I come back out, raising it over my head in victory.

"Got it! Okay, I'm just gonna . . ." I look over my shoulder and jerk my head in the direction of my tent.

"You move so fast," she says.

Her voice is so low it's almost inaudible, but I stop.

"Huh?"

"You're like a sped-up audiobook." She searches my face and rubs at her eyes sleepily. "I can mostly follow what you're saying, but sometimes I think I must be missing some of the nuance."

My heart sinks. This is it. I don't even get the weekend before things go south. She's annoyed with me; I've been too much of myself.

"Sorry," I start. I clench my fists over the silvery straps of my Birkenstocks. My leg starts bouncing of its own accord. "It's totally okay, I get it. This happens sometimes. Me and my big mouth, you know what I mean? Always running . . ."

"Sorry? For what? People have to work to keep up with you, you know?" She sets her guitar down gently into her hard case and rubs her hands down her bare thighs before sliding them into the pockets of her red Indiana men's basketball hoodie. *Oh my God how did I not notice how short her sleep shorts were?*

She scratches the back of her neck as she stands up.

"I just mean, um, you're the kind of person who takes work to understand." She looks up at me and I want to cry a little at how earnest she looks. "I'm saying you're worth the work, Olivia.

"Anyway, um"—she looks away before straightening her spine and smiling, just a little—"you want to grab breakfast and showers before we head in?"

I'm saying you're worth the work, Olivia. I don't know what to say to that, but those seven words are marching straight into my brain and taking up residence where just a few seconds ago lived insecurity. If she wants to do the work for me, I can do the same for her.

I shake my head. I don't want to go back and change or eat or leave, period. I want to practice. I want us to be so good that there's no way we could mess this up. I want to prove Toni right about me. I want to have walked into her life and made it better and walk away without being shattered. It has to be possible, otherwise I don't know what I'm doing. I don't know what hope there is for someone like me if I try my best and still end up ruining everything.

When my mom got her master's through night classes and got her job as an administrator at Park Meade, it was supposed to change our lives. It got me and Nia seriously lowered tuition to one of the best high schools in the state, it got us out of our shitty two-bedroom on the east side of town and into a cute little house near Broad Ripple. It got Nia into Harvard, and my mom the respectable white-collar job she'd always wanted. I could put on the requisite pleated uniform skirt and the gray-and-red Park Meade cardigan, but no outfit could ever dress me up enough to hide who I really am.

The faulty piece was always going to be me. Over and over again, mediocre test scores, more interest in punk shows than Key Club, too many dates and hookups and heartbreaks to count. And then the pictures of me that were never supposed to get out, and the scandal, and the star basketball player whose entire future now hinges on whether or not I testify against him in a few days. The embarrassment of a family and the ruined career of a boy with more potential in his pinky finger than most people have in their whole bodies all comes down to me.

So, if I only get one chance, this girl's life will be better for having had me in it. That's all I want.

"We should rehearse." I point to Toni's guitar case, where it leans against her truck. "Can we try it from the bridge first? I think I'm coming in flat on the fast part."

Toni looks at me for a second before she sits back down. She hesitates, but eventually nods.

"Okay," she says. "Let's do it."

TONI

SATURDAY MORNING

We practice for so long my voice feels a little raw by the time we decide to take a break. Thank God for Olivia's short but spectacular stint in chorus, because I think we sound good together. Really good. Her voice is a little lighter than mine, something delicate, but we weave together like two halves of a whole.

By the time we're finished, nearly two hours have passed, and I didn't even notice. Peter bounds over to us, his hair pulled back in the same loose man bun that he insists makes him look like *the brown Brad Pitt*, while Imani lags behind him, arms crossed as usual. I've never seen someone so committed to keeping their arms firmly locked in that position. It's honestly impressive.

The two of them both look ready to go, unlike me and Olivia. Peter shifts his eyes back and forth between the two of us, still a little worse for wear from practicing all morning instead of getting ready.

"Well aren't you two just a sight for sore eyes?" he says, arms wide. "Bestie and future bestie—I've decided we're going to be best friends, by the way, just so that's on the record—you both need to get yourselves together. DJ Louddoc goes on in thirty!"

It's still before noon since me and Olivia had a bigger head start to our day than anyone around us. Peter looks like freshly canned sunshine, all smiles while telling a bland-faced Imani how John Quincy Adams used to skinny-dip in the Potomac—one of his favorite factoids.

I'd probably be smiling too if I'd managed more than a few winks of sleep last night. Having Olivia next to me all night left me buzzing. I couldn't relax knowing how close her body was to mine, how when she turned on her side, I could feel small puffs of her breath on my neck. It's like I couldn't tune anything out. The warmth of her, the soft sound of her snores—all of it made for an impossible sleep situation. So I woke up at the crack of dawn and decided to pick up my guitar. It didn't feel as alive as it had the night before when I was playing with and for Olivia, but it felt good. It felt better than it had in eight months.

"You two need to get dressed!" He points at Olivia and me. I don't bother to note that he's still wearing his clothes from the day before, so he doesn't have much room to talk.

Imani rolls her eyes and adds, "I refuse to miss this DJ after Peter has talked about him all morning. I need to be able to hold it over his head if he actually sucks."

Peter looks absolutely smitten as he responds, "No way, don't turn this around on me. You totally want to see him too."

"Liv?" Imani ignores Peter in favor of turning to Olivia, and I realize then that she hasn't spoken since the two walked up. She's biting her lip and flipping her phone over in her hand, almost nervously. I think about asking what's wrong, but she snaps out of it. She looks up at our friends as if seeing them for the first time, and smiles.

And if nobody else notices how fake it looks, then who am I to mention it?

We make it into the Core just in the nick of time for the set to start.

"We have just enough time to run through the song a few more times after this," Olivia says, her voice raising to be heard above the reverb coming from the massive speakers behind us. She squeezes my shoulder like I need reassuring. "It'll be great."

Her voice is drowned out by the wave of people carrying the four of us farther and farther into the fray—the telltale sign that a set is getting ready to start. It's the same thing I've been swept into hundreds of times over the course of my life, at over a dozen Farmlands, but with her next to me, it's unimaginably different.

Olivia is practically bouncing on the balls of her feet as we wait.

We all get a notification on our phones with a clue for the next apple, but it's the one Olivia found in the barn last night. Knowing that we're ahead of the game makes me feel looser, a little more free.

Peter is talking to my left, going on about his dead presidents obsession in the way that I just find endearing now—"Did you know James K. Polk banned dancing from the White House? It was like *Footloose!*"—as Imani nods along distractedly. It feels good, standing between my best friend and Olivia even though I'm still not sure, exactly, who she is to me. I just know that whatever we are to each other is working. That I feel excited about something—about someone.

"You guys, this is too good," Olivia says over the low roar of crowd noise. She smiles at the three of us and holds up her camera. "Everyone, squeeze together!"

She holds it up to her face and aims it in me and Peter's direction. Peter is quick to pose, his weight leaning into mine, his tongue out and hang loose sign at the ready. It's so *him* that my laugh bubbles out before I can even think to stop it. Even Imani offers a tentative quirk of her lips, on her tiptoes to be seen over Peter's shoulder.

The flash comes so quickly, I'm still laughing even after Olivia pulls the film from the camera and holds it up as she waits for the photo to emerge. When it does, I feel something bubbling up inside that seems dangerously close to *really damn happy*.

I feel almost outside myself—like the last eight months of my life haven't disappeared exactly, but that the sharpness of their edges has rounded enough for me to breathe. I'm back in my favorite place on earth, and the sensation of being surrounded by people who love music as much as I do is almost overwhelming. There's an energy buzzing in my hands and feet that feels boundless in its sudden intensity. I want to play my guitar, and dance, put my arms around Olivia, and scream at the top of my lungs all at the same time. Bodies are pressing in from all sides, and instead of it feeling claustrophobic, it's a welcome embrace.

Peter throws an arm around my shoulder, and I don't roll my eyes and shake it off. I don't even want to. Instead, I wrap an arm around his waist and give him a quick squeeze. Olivia's bare arm brushes against mine, and I feel the rush of that feeling everywhere.

I've always heard people say things can be *electric*, but I didn't understand it until this moment.

I wonder what my old classmates would think about the snapshots of me from this weekend if they ever saw them. I can imagine it now. Me smiling down at a buoyant, beautiful girl. Peter with an arm around my neck, making some kind of ridiculous face at the camera. The four of us taking gulps from our water bottles at the same time and laughing when we realize how in sync we are. To see me in this moment would be to see a version of me that no one from Ardsley Academy has ever seen before.

I feel so far away from that Toni right now.

"It's perfect," Olivia says, handing me the photo. I look down at her and think about what a strange and wonderful twist of fate that full sign-up sheet and stupid scavenger hunt turned out to be.

"Nothing's perfect," I say, Toni the ice queen slipping through somehow. I don't even mean it. I hand the picture back even though I want to keep it, keep this, forever.

"I disagree." Like she's read my mind, she unzips the fanny pack around my waist and slips the photo inside. "This." She zips it shut and looks up at me. She smiles so small and sweet it takes everything in me not to mess things up by wanting more like I almost had last night. "Is perfect."

Peter drops his arm from my neck and cups his hands around his mouth to cheer. Everyone else starts whistling and shouting, and I know that means DJ Louddoc must be coming out on stage, even though I can barely see over the mass of bodies in front of me.

When I see freedom, I see a stage, the beginning moments of a show, the slow rise of the lights and the burgeoning hum of an audience welcoming their favorite artist into the space. In this moment, I am the audience. This time last year, I was imagining myself from the stage, looking out into the faces of people who wanted nothing more than what I wanted: to be both grounded and lifted away all at once.

But then my dad died—was *taken* from me—and I hadn't picked up my guitar again until last night. Until I played for Olivia, and then spent the rest of the night and this morning playing *with* her. And things felt right, like my body was mine again, completely at ease. The gut-churning anxiety that had been roiling for months, for years probably, if I'm being honest, was gone.

"Are you ready?" Olivia turns to me and shouts over the music. She pushes her heart-shaped sunglasses up into her hair and smiles. I am ready, I think. Maybe I've always been ready for this and didn't even know it. The crowd starts moving forward, shuffling us around, and their screams are getting louder and more insistent as DJ Louddoc sets up and I'm looking at her and she's looking back at me and my heart's a marching band, big and brash and impossible to ignore and in that moment—

I almost don't hear the bang.

My dad was shot to death in a gas station robbery gone wrong.

We were on our way to Indy Classics, the music shop near my house. He had only been home from tour for an hour when we left, but he yawned and slid his feet into his boots, grabbed his coat, and wrestled me for the keys to his pickup before we got in the truck. The pickup is old, and doesn't have an aux input, so he thumped his hands against the wheel as he drove and tried to get me to find the harmony in an old Loretta Lynn song he was singing.

I needed sheet music. I didn't need it so much as I just wanted it. Or, I didn't want it so much as I wanted to spend time with my dad and knew that if I told him I needed it, he would abandon the nap he was planning to take before my mom got home and drive me to the store instead. I wanted to spend time with him but I had no way of knowing that we'd stop and that stop would be the last one he'd ever take and—fuck.

Let's try this again.

My dad was in the wrong place at the wrong time—in a country where anyplace and anytime can be the wrong one.

Classics is exactly two and three-quarter miles from my house. I know that now, even if I didn't know it then. At exactly one-and-a-half miles from my house, there's a Shell gas station that sits short and squat back off the main road. It is dingy. The lighting is poor—the parking lot half-glowing under a single, flickering lamppost and a buzzing bulb over one of the two gas pumps. It is not the type of place you should go in by yourself at night.

I know that now too, even if I didn't know that then.

"Oh man, let me run in here real quick! I have been craving some Hot Chips. You know how hard those things are to find on the road?" He turned off the street and into the parking lot with a broad smile. He reached over and tugged at one of my locs before turning up the heat. "Don't freeze to death while I'm in there, alright?"

I smiled and reached over to run a hand over his bald head—our usual exchange. He had locs like mine once upon a time, back in the day. I wasn't old enough to remember them, but they're right there in his picture from Farmland, his long hair pulled back into a low ponytail as he smiles next to Anthony Kiedis. His face was without lines in that picture, just a slight crinkle around his eyes when he smiled. His smile never changed, but his face eventually did.

When I looked at him in the low light of that parking lot, he looked tired. Like maybe the road was taking the same toll on him that it was taking on me and Mom.

"I could've sent you some Hot Chips, Dad," I said as he pushed open his door. A rush of cold air swept the cab, and I shivered. He looked at me and said with a wink, "Nah, kid. Finally getting the things I miss while I'm away makes coming home even better.

"It'll only take a second, I promise!" He shouted as he jogged inside.

I did not think to stop him as he climbed out of the truck and shut the door. I did not think that his desire for his favorite snack food and my desire to spend time with him could be mistakes. I didn't think of anything except how glad I was that he was home, and how eager I was to find a way to keep him.

I did not pay attention as the man in the hoodie walked in.

I did not see him as he held a gun up to the cashier and demanded the money in the register.

I did not watch as my dad tried to intervene.

But I heard the gunshot.

I saw my dad hit the linoleum floor through the dingy glass, and the man in the hoodie run out into the night, stolen money no doubt tucked into his pockets.

I don't remember stumbling out the door, or falling to my knees next to his body, blood soaking my faded black jeans, or screaming as the cashier fumbled with his phone and finally called the police. I don't remember running into the parking lot after the ambulance that hauled my dad's body away. These are things I only know because I was told. The rest of the night comes and goes in flashes.

But I see it all clearly now—the images flit in front of me like a highlight reel of the worst night of my life. My ears are ringing, and I can't breathe, and the tips of my fingers are tingling like even my blood has forgotten how to circulate properly. My mouth tastes like copper. There's a hand on my face and someone in my ear whispering, *Come back to me. You're okay. You're alright. Come back to me. You're safe. I promise.*

OLIVIA

SATURDAY AFTERNOON

I don't know what's going on or why Toni has suddenly gone stock-still next to me, but I'm freaking the hell out. I can't even hear whatever DJ Louddoc is playing now because all I can think about is helping Toni. Her breath is coming in small, tight-sounding hiccups and it's so much like an asthma attack I instinctively reach for my inhaler to hand over. I realize it's not that though, because I've never had an asthma attack make me go as glassy-eyed as she is right now.

I manage to push our way out of the crowd, her hand in mine as I not-so-politely elbow people out of the way until I can ease her to the ground and settle her against a tree. I don't know what happened, I'm not sure what to do, and Toni's eyes are closed now like she's completely vacated her body, so I do the only thing I know how to do. I talk.

I hold on to Toni's biceps and repeat a mantra of, more than anything else, wishful thinking. "Come back to me. You're okay. You're alright. Come back to me. You're safe. I promise. You're at Farmland. You're with me, remember? Bad things don't happen at Farmland. You're gonna be fine. I swear." I say it with as much ferocity as I can muster, as if my belief in what I'm saying alone is enough to make it true.

Her breath starts slowing down, her chest rising and falling more evenly, but she's still not back to normal.

I slide my hands down her arms to hers. I link our fingers together. I squeeze just this side of tight enough to bring her back, here, to this moment, with me.

When she finally meets my eyes, it's like she doesn't recognize me. Or, well, not that exactly. It's more like she's seeing me for the first time. I don't know what to make of it, all I know is how relieved I am to have her back.

"Toni!" Peter runs up to us, Imani trailing just behind him. His hair falls out of the lazy half-bun he has it in and flies around his face as he kneels down before Toni. "I didn't know where you guys went. I'm sorry, dude. I forgot about the sound effects. I should have known. I should've warned you. I didn't even think."

He hugs her like it's second nature, and Toni practically falls into him. She tucks her face into his shoulder, and he murmurs something that I can't hear. Toni nods, just once, and he pulls back but keeps his hands on her shoulders.

"Known what?" I look between the two of them, but Toni refuses to look at me. "Peter, what happened?"

My instincts scream: *What did I do?*

"Nothing." It's the first thing I've heard her say since the set started, and it comes out low and gruff. "This isn't—" She stops herself and rubs a hand over her face. "I can't do this."

"Can't do what?" I'm missing something and I don't know what it is.

Peter and Toni seem to communicate wordlessly again, and Peter is the one to answer. He squeezes my shoulder and for the first time since we've met, looks genuinely sad. He helps Toni to her feet and looks down at me with a frown.

"Sorry, Olivia. I think this might be the end of the road."

The two of them walk away, and Toni looks absolutely wrecked as she leaves. There's tension in every inch of her body, and it's all wrong. I don't know what happened or what's happening now and I want to go back to this morning when it seemed like things were working out and me and Toni were on the same wavelength—the rightness of the way our voices sounded together still covering me like a blanket.

I have to go after her.

"Olivia, wait! What are you doing? Didn't you hear her?" Imani jogs to catch up with me and plants herself in my way. "She wants to be left alone. She practically said she doesn't want you around!"

"Of course I heard her!" But the string of this weekend, of all the *good* that seemed to be weaving together, is unraveling before my eyes and I don't even know why. "Which is why I have to go after her. If she leaves, all this—all weekend—was for nothing."

I don't know what Imani's upset about, but then again, I feel like I never know anymore. I can't seem to do anything right in her eyes. Despite the fact that maybe she didn't want to come to this festival originally—but look what it got her! She hasn't ignored Peter all morning, has even smiled at him a few times, which for Imani is like offering someone her hand in marriage. *I* did that. But she doesn't even care.

I don't have to figure it out though. Every second I stand here arguing with Imani is a second that Toni could be scared, or hurting, or—I don't even know. I should be there for her. It feels like more than an obligation of our deal now. Somewhere between the moment she patched my foot up and the moment she smiled a smile so beautiful for that snapshot that I knew I could give her the photo and I'd still never be able to get that look out of my head, Toni became someone I'm scared to lose.

And not in the temporary way I'm used to either. Not the way I felt about June or Katie or Jared or Moira or Nick, people I clung to because of what they could make me feel about myself for however long they had their eyes on me—because I was scared of what it meant to be a person they didn't want. I don't want to lose

Toni because when she looks at me, I don't see someone who can fix me; I see someone who believes I don't need fixing.

I can see Peter and Toni getting smaller and smaller as they move away, and I step to the right to try and get around her, but Imani stands in my way again.

"You made me a promise." She tilts her head up defiantly and points at my chest. "You pinky swore, Olivia. Since when do we break those?"

She has to understand. I need her to get that I'm not doing what I usually do. This isn't about me wanting to kiss and date and spend the rest of my life with Toni. This isn't some fantasy. This is bigger than my dreams of storybook romances. For once, I need *her* to trust *me*.

"You've been following after her all weekend, Olivia. And I tried not to blow this for you because it seemed important, but—" Her face twists, and I can see it hitting her. The way I've spent more and more time with Toni, even when I didn't have to. The fact that I didn't even try to fight Peter for my sleeping bag and tent last night. "This isn't about the competition or that stupid scavenger hunt anymore." She closes her eyes and lowers her voice so much I can barely hear it. "You *promised* me."

I feel her disappointment like a blow to my chest. There's nothing more sacred between us than our promises.

"And you say you aren't hiding anything about the hearing. But you are." She rubs her thumb over her pinky ring and her voice gets a little brittle. "I know you are."

I don't answer, because I know telling her the truth will ruin everything. I can't salvage what happened with Troy. But if I keep quiet, I can keep things from getting worse.

I want so badly for her to get it, so I grab her hands and squeeze. This isn't like all the other times. This isn't like Troy. This is me, no costumes and no gimmicks to get Toni to pay attention to me, and she seems to like me anyway. I can't mess this up, because I think this could be real.

"And I made *her* a promise, too, Mani. I have to fix this. I can fix this."

I try to ignore the look of betrayal on my best friend's face as I walk away.

TONI

SATURDAY AFTERNOON

"T, you gotta tell her," Peter says. He hands me a frozen lemonade from a nearby food stand and urges me to drink it. "You can't run from this. I don't think you even really want to, to be honest."

We made it to the other side of the Core before I finally felt okay to just sit down again, like there was some invisible string tying me to the worst panic attack I'd had in months that could snap if I just walked far enough. I pull my knees up to my neck and rest my chin on them. I need to get my bearings. I need to figure my shit out. I'm all over the place right now.

Peter is right. I need to face whatever it is I'm running from: The fact that my entire future is up in the air, the fact that I miss my dad so much it feels like it's going to crush me, the fact that I want Olivia more than I've ever wanted another person and I have no idea what to do with that. But I don't even know where to start.

"What if I do?" I ask. Peter sits cross-legged in front of me, waiting me out. For someone who talks so much, he's surprisingly good at silence when it counts. "What if I'm not cut out for this? What if all I'm good for is leaving?"

Like my dad goes unsaid between us.

I want to trust Olivia, and that scares me. I've never wanted that with anyone before. And giving her this, telling her about my dad, is as close as I can allow her to be to me. Losing him a final time after losing him time and time again to a tour or to playing in someone's studio session over the course of my life is an open wound. Will always be an open wound.

When you open yourself up to someone, when they know your most vulnerable parts, what's to keep them from hurting you? When I finally say all this out loud, I realize it's the first time in my life I've ever admitted to another person why I am the way I am. Why I push away instead of pull closer, why I retreat instead of advance.

"I think you gotta start asking who you're really protecting by lying to yourself, you know?" he asks. He yanks some grass out of the ground and sprinkles it on top of my boots. "Cause the way I see it, the running hurts more than the standing still. And besides." He grins. "You let me in. And look how that worked out."

And like he summoned her by saying her name, I hear Olivia's voice before I see her face, and I can tell just by the sound of it she ran to catch up with us. I feel guilty, especially considering how bad her asthma has been in this humidity, but I can't bring myself to look up at her. I'm mortified.

No one has ever seen me like that, fighting my way back from a panic attack, except for Peter and my mom. I didn't used to have them. They started after my dad died, and have occurred more often and more intensely for the past few months. Anything can trigger it: from something as extreme as a car backfiring that sounds too much like a gunshot, to something as simple as hearing a song that reminds me of him.

It's like I've been trying to hold my life together with both hands, but they're shaking too much to maintain a decent grip. When I have a panic attack, it's me at my weakest, at my most fragile. I vowed I was never going to let anyone see me without my guard up, ever. It's the only way I've managed to protect myself for as long as I have. But I couldn't this time. And not only that, but Olivia managed to bring me back to the surface quicker than I've ever been able to on my own.

I already need her too much. That's not going to work.

"I'm gonna just . . . Um, grab something over . . . there." Peter scampers off like a bug and I make a mental note to crush him like one when he comes back. Some best friend he is.

Olivia holds her hands out. "We had a deal, remember?"

I don't mention the fact that I've already violated my side of the deal, including the unspoken half. I was supposed to help her find these apples, and maintain as much distance as possible, and we were supposed to go our separate ways at the end of the weekend completely unscathed. But I messed up. She told me this was nothing but a business deal, and I said the same, and I lied.

"Yeah, well, I'm relieving you of your end of the bargain." I look up at her face. She's taken off the massive heart-shaped sunglasses I'll now never be able to separate from her. Her expression is gentle, curious. "Consider it canceled. Null and void. Cool?"

Her face changes from soft and sympathetic to something harder almost instantly.

"No. That's actually not *cool*, Toni. It's the opposite of cool. The very definition of uncool, in fact." She sits down next to me and tucks her legs underneath her body. She sighs. "I'm not talking about the competition. I'm talking about last night, at the barn. You agreed to trust me."

'Cause the way I see it, the running hurts more than the standing still.

She's right. All I have is my word, so I tell her. And I keep telling her. And I don't stop talking until it's all out, the entire mess of a story. The night my dad died. The freshman year I'm scheduled to start in two days. The fact that I have no idea what I want from my life and I'm terrified that the music isn't going to be enough to help me figure it out anymore. Why the Golden Apple feels like the key.

"I think we should start over," she says once I finish. "I'm Olivia

Brooks. I'm sixteen years old. I'm from Indianapolis, Indiana. I'm about to be a senior at the worst high school in the history of all high schools. I'm aggressively asthmatic. And I'm allergic to shellfish."

She holds her hand out, and I don't really understand what's happening, but I shake it.

"Worst high school in the history of high schools. That's a big title."

She smiles. "I mean it. Hell is empty and all the devils are at Park Meade High School."

I nod. This is her olive branch to me, a clean slate.

"Antonia Jackson Foster. Toni to most people, TJ sometimes. I'm seventeen but I'll be eighteen in a week. I'm also from Indy and I'm not allergic to anything. But sometimes I say I'm allergic to onions so that they don't end up anywhere near my food. And I graduated from Ardsley Academy two months ago." Her eyes widen immediately, and I smirk. "So, technically, we're rivals. Go Blue Devils."

"Nice to meet you, Toni." She finally slips her hand from mine then and presses her lips together in thought. "Look, I'm not going to force you—honestly, knowing what I know now, I can't believe you wanted to do this in the first place—but I would still like to compete together today if you're willing."

I think about saying no, about walking away, about never feeling again the way that I felt last night, playing my dad's song under the stars with Olivia—even if it doesn't mean the same thing to her as it does to me. And I know that it's just not an option.

"Melodrama aside"—I push myself to standing and hold out my hand—"I would like that too."

When she grabs my hand and pulls herself up to standing as well, it feels like what's in front of me is finally solid instead of in constant motion. It feels like settling.

"Well, Toni Foster from Ardsley Academy, we better hurry up." She tugs me in the direction of the exit, toward the campgrounds where my guitar currently waits. "I think there's a stage with our name on it."

If I thought I was panicking before, it's nothing like the cold-bucket-of-water-like realization that we have less than twenty minutes to get changed, grab my guitar, and make it back to the performance barn in time for our slot. Olivia seems to be taking it all in stride though. And by that I mean she's no more frenetic about our preparation as she is about anything else, which isn't saying all that much.

We sprint from the Core to the campsite. When we get there, I grab my dad's case out of the truck and start back in the direction of the barn before Olivia says, "Wait a second. Are you planning on wearing that?"

I look down at my outfit, confused. I'm wearing a solid black racerback tank top, slightly stained around the collar from my sweat, a pair of faded cutoffs with uneven hems because I got too lazy to fix them, and my cowboy boots. Some might even say I look festival-chic. But Olivia shakes her head in disbelief. She ducks into the tent and rustles around like she owns the place.

"What's wrong with this?" I ask, and if I sound a little indignant who cares? "They care about the music, not how we look."

"The hot ones always say that!" She shouts from inside, and I'm glad she can't see how much those six words just affected me. *Focus, Foster.*

"Here!" She tosses a bundle of clothes at me and rushes me into the tent to get changed. "Go, go!"

And because Olivia is the type of person you can't help but pay attention to, can't help but listen to, we swap places and I get dressed. It's the quickest of all costume changes.

So fast that I don't even realize I'm wearing one of Peter's shirts. It's an authentic bleach-stained Nirvana tour tee from 1993—the one from the In Utero tour with the angel on the front—that he found on eBay and cut into a crop top at the beginning of the summer. I'm also wearing a pair of my own shorts, but they're the high-waist, black denim kind with frayed ends that make my legs looks even longer than they already are.

When I step out, Olivia reaches for me and takes the bandana that's been around my forehead all day and ties it around my neck. I let her fuss, and try to ignore the wave of warmth that rushes over me as she lets my hair down from its bun and situates my wide-brimmed hat on top of my locs.

"There." She steps back and smiles. I don't even have to look at myself to know what she's managed to pull together and to know that I like it. It's something I'm comfortable in, that looks natural on me, but with a spin. "Just because you've got substance doesn't mean you can't give a little flair too. Now they have no reason to second-guess you."

Everything I've been fighting back since yesterday threatens to spill over in that moment, but there's no time. She grabs the guitar case and shoves it into my hand and then we're off, running back to the Core.

Luckily, it's still early afternoon, so the rush to get in has calmed and the line moves quicker than it has all weekend. I have to thank the festival gods for the good fortune as we make our way through security—with a haphazard check of my dad's case to make sure nothing is inside it other than my guitar—and rush through the Core to the performance barn. Our phones buzz with a message from Peter saying he and Imani are in the audience and wishing us luck, just as we burst into the backstage area.

"Toni Jackson and Olivia Brooks?" A tech with a huge headset asks just as the audience bursts into applause to welcome another duo on stage. It's two white women who look like they just walked straight out of a Free People, and I'm suddenly even more grateful Olivia suggested I switch up my look for this. These people came camera-ready.

We nod. "Great, you're on next." And without any other fanfare, he's off.

"You ready?" I ask Olivia once the tech is gone.

Her smile is a little wobbly as she nods, wordlessly.

Before I can ask after her new expression, a voice behind us cuts in, "Toni?"

I turn to see a familiar head of red hair flying toward me as she immediately pulls me in for a half hug. She looks mostly the same as the last time I saw her, but her hair is slightly longer and a new tattoo has cropped up on her forearm that reads: *I am deliberate and afraid of nothing.*

"Mack?" I break into a smile. And I know she's surprised to see it, because her eyebrows go straight up as she shoots me one back. "What are you doing here?"

I stand back to appraise her for a second, happy to see her and surprised by my own surprise. Mack is Davey Mack's—or David McCarthy, as his Wikipedia page would tell you—younger cousin, but the two have always been more like siblings. So much so that every summer since I was thirteen and she was fourteen, she's tagged along with Kittredge for a few Midwestern tour dates.

We met a few years ago when the band was playing Lollapalooza. The two of us were the only under-eighteens backstage, so we bonded over our shared love of Sheila E. and watched YouTube videos in the greenroom while we waited for the show to be over. I wouldn't necessarily call her a friend, but there were very few people who got what it was like, in that specific way, to be a part of the Kittredge machine than another newly minted teenager.

"I was back with the band for a few dates again this summer. Great, right? Can't believe Davey hasn't gotten sick of me yet, but here I am!" She holds her arms wide, revealing her KITTREDGE "BACK WHERE WE BELONG" 2021 NORTH AMERICAN TOUR tank top. A volunteer shushes her when her voice raises, and she tries (and mostly fails) to lower it so as not to disturb the act on stage. "You're competing?"

I shrug, a little embarrassed. I don't know why, it's not like it's anything to be ashamed of, just that I'm still not sure how this is going to go. Still not sure I can do this in front of anyone other than Olivia.

And then I realize that Olivia's just been standing off to the side, looking between the two of us with this vaguely confused look on her face.

"Oh! Hey, Olivia"—I hold my arm out and wave her closer—"this is Mack McCarthy. She's Davey Mack's cousin. We used to hang out when we were younger, back when my dad worked for Kittredge."

Olivia offers a hand and Mack shakes it with her usual level of vigor.

"Nice to meet you, Olivia!" Mack whisper-shouts. She gives us a quick salute. She leans in, "I'm headed out to the audience, but Toni, you should text me!"

She holds her palm out and up for my phone and I hand it over to her. She types in her number and shoots herself a text so I'll have hers too. And as soon as she jogs off, a volunteer with a clip-board walks up to tell us we're on next.

"Your friend was . . . nice."

Olivia looks a little green after they walk away. I can't even focus on Mack right now. All I see is the way Olivia's bouncing her leg and cutting her eyes between me and the stage. I didn't even think about the fact that she might be the type of person with stage fright, given her general sunniness, but I don't mind the idea of comforting her. In fact, I want to.

I want to tell her it's going to be okay and that no matter what happens on that stage, I'm glad that we did this. I'm glad that she fell into that tent and needed help with some gimmicky scavenger hunt and I'm glad she didn't run away when I tried to get her to. I'm glad she stayed. But I don't have the language for all of that yet. No words to describe how much her presence has meant to me.

So I trust my gut. I grab her hand and squeeze. I don't know where Olivia's set her camera, but I take a mental picture of the way the light from the stage halos her head from behind.

My dad was right about a lot of things, but when I look at her, when I think about how I felt last night playing in front of her, I know I don't need to go on stage to figure out what to do next. I lean forward, close my eyes, and follow my own Truth.

OLIVIA

SATURDAY AFTERNOON

My mind is reeling and I'm doing my best to keep from losing whatever cool I've managed to fake thus far, but I'm quickly unraveling. Did I maybe stretch the truth about how comfortable I am performing in public? Maybe. But that was manageable until that—admittedly cute if a little awkward—Mack girl came over and made Toni do that smile I've only seen her do once before.

Does it mean something? Are they just really cordial exes? Toni did say they used to hang out, but maybe that's just cool roadie code for *We definitely used to hook up.* I mean, it's not like she's explicitly said that there's anything going on here besides a few stolen moments that could've meant something but could be denied if pressed.

I know it shouldn't matter, that it's none of my business, that I'm the one who made it a point not to kiss her last night, but I'm suddenly buzzing with jealousy. It sits low in my belly and snakes its way through my entire body.

My knee bounces and a familiar prickle starts creeping across my skin. I try to rationalize it away, remind myself that it doesn't matter, that me and Toni are *good*, that we've had a great time together over the past two days. But I can't stop thinking about what I might be missing. I'm just me, haven't given her anything but the unbridled version of myself. What if it's not enough? What if all she needed was a reminder from her past to push her toward the exit?

"Olivia?" My head snaps up.

My brain was skyrocketing to nowhere good, and I've been there a thousand times before. But Toni squeezes my hand gently, our only point of contact, and brings me back down to earth. Her face is soft and her smile is different than any of the others we've shared so far. It's the type of smile that tells me I'm already too far gone for my own good. That despite my best efforts—and I do mean the very best I've ever given—there's no way this weekend ends without me losing just a bit of myself in this thing between us.

It's enough to make the questions disappear.

"Yeah?"

"Can I . . ."

And it's like the dance barn all over again, only this time, it's better. I'm not wondering whether or not I'm making the right choice, I'm not second-guessing myself. We made it here. We did this.

I don't even shut my eyes as I lean in to meet her lips. I don't want to miss any of this. It feels like the first time—like the way a first kiss should be. Palms sweaty and so, so soft. Noses brushing just this side of awkward. It's so much and not enough and it's over too soon.

She pulls back and smiles.

"I just had to do that before we went out there," she says. I bob my head up and down because I'm pretty sure if I tried to speak it would come out as gibberish right now. Her eyebrows are slightly raised and she's biting her lip and *God, how is it fair that one person is that cute?* "Thank you. For everything."

We won't find out about whether or not we won until tomorrow morning, so I want to tell her to hold her thank-you until then. The pair in front of us finishes and the audience gives them modest applause. I didn't even hear any of their performance. This is it. My heart feels like it's lodged in my esophagus, so I reach for my inhaler on instinct, even though I'm breathing fine.

I don't have time to take a panic puff before they're calling us out though. The guy who's emceeing calls out our names—he says *Toni Jackson*, her first and middle instead of first and last, and I can't help but think that her name even sounds like a star in the making—and the crowd starts to applaud and then we're out.

The sounds of clapping are overwhelming, even though I can

see through the bright spotlights they have on us that there can't be more than two hundred people in the barn. My palms start sweating, and I bring my hand up to my brow line to shield my eyes from the lights. Is it supposed to be this hot up here? Can they turn the freaking lights down a little?

Unlike me, Toni waves comfortably, her smile back on her face and completely at ease. Out here, it doesn't seem like she has any problem warming up to people. She looks at home, like this is exactly where she's supposed to be, surrounded by music.

And suddenly, I'm ridiculously, overwhelmingly nervous. In true Olivia Brooks style, I didn't think about what all this would entail when I jumped straight into it. I saw an opportunity and I took it. And now I'm looking into the crowd and the lead singers of Sonny Blue *and* Kittredge, two of the headlining bands and two of the biggest artists in the world, are there to watch me crash and burn. But what's worse, I'm going to crash and burn and bring Toni down with me. My heart is beating a little too fast and I feel like I'm breathing the way I only do after running from the cops at a house party—nerves and a sense of danger shooting up my spine.

I'm going to ruin her dream. I'm going to mess up her life just like I have every other person who's ever gotten close to me.

My eyes practically bug out of my head as I look at Toni.

"That's—that's Bonnie Harrison out there. And Davey Mack," I whisper and cover the mic so it can't pick up any of the sound. My heartbeat is out of control and I reach for my inhaler. I take a puff, partially because my breath starts coming in shorter, but also because it buys me some time. This is *crazy*. "I can't do this, Toni. I'm sorry, I'm so sorry but I seriously can't—"

Toni swings her guitar to her back and stands so her back is to the audience. Her hat even manages to block the spotlight as she positions herself in front of me. She looks my face over, considering, before placing her hands on both of my cheeks.

I stop breathing again, but this time for a completely different reason. Her smile isn't the kind that I'm used to. The kind that Troy used to flash, or Casey or Liza or Andi—a little like I was something to be devoured, a prize to be won. One that said: *I'm watching you, I'm picking you apart.*

It's so kind and so solid and somehow so *her* that I relax.

"You know how you told me you you're good at being who people want you to be?"

I open my mouth and immediately try to backtrack. I thought we cleared this up earlier. I don't want her to think that this— whatever is happening between the two of us—is anything like that. She's special. *This* is special.

"Toni, I didn't—"

"Hear me out, okay?" She shakes her head briefly. I can hear the crowd murmuring behind her, and I try to block out all the noise. I try to direct my focus entirely on the girl in front of me. "Just look at me the whole time. Forget them. Just look right at me. Be the person you have been when it's just the two of us, alright? They won't be able to help but feel the way I do when I'm with you."

TONI

SATURDAY AFTERNOON

I haven't played in front of anyone but Olivia in eight months. Three days ago, I was still halfway convinced I would never play again. But when I sit back on my stool and start strumming, I follow the advice I gave Olivia and look directly at her.

Right now, there is no audience, no Davey Mack or Bonnie Harrison judging our every move. There are no massive life decisions to be made soon, no contest to win or scavenger hunt to complete. There's just Olivia. There is just the girl who's made me feel more alive in the past twenty-four hours than I have in my entire life, made me want to take more chances than I ever have before, singing along with me.

I knew her voice was good before from our brief rehearsals, but right now it sounds perfect—so clear and silvery. This is more than a song. How I feel? This is music. This is everything.

Everything feels so natural, and with Olivia in front of me, returning to my music feels just like riding a bike. I'm in the basement with my dad as he taught me to play "Seven Nation Army" on his Gibson SG. I'm in the car with him listening to Sonny Blue demos through the truck's old speakers. I'm on his shoulders at my first Farmland. And for the first time in a long time, the thought of my dad doesn't threaten to drown me, it buoys me. We might not have gotten all the time I wanted, but we'll always have this, these chords that bind us.

And before I know it, I'm playing the final notes of the song, and Olivia is standing up from her stool, and I'm turning to wave at the audience, and watching the panel of judges—Davey Mack, Pop Top, and Bonnie Harrison—grin in my direction, and then I'm trailing Olivia offstage.

The rush of the magnitude of what just happened hits me the minute we get back in the wings. We did it. This is real.

I barely stop to set my guitar back down in its case, in such a rush to get to Olivia. When I finally do, I grab her hand and turn her to face me, because at this point it would require some almost-Herculean restraint to make it possible to stop wanting to be close to her and I'm just not sure I have it in me anymore.

"We did it. You—how are you even real?"

I don't know who kissed whom, but suddenly my lips are

pressed to hers with no finesse whatsoever and I can't imagine stopping. This one is different than the kiss before we went on stage, all reserved and soft. I feel like I could explode from this.

Kissing Olivia is like a revelation. I don't know how I had a life before I kissed her. I don't know how I'll have a life without kissing her, once this is all over. I want to do it again and again. And then I realize: I can.

I'm dizzy at the thought of it. I can *kiss her*. I can wrap my arms around her and pull her to me and press so close that we're practically sharing breath and it's not just tolerated, but welcomed.

So I do it again. And again. And then I'm a little light-headed because, truth be told, this is something that I never thought to study. It's not like learning a new song, where I can tell you what notes belong where and why and what they mean in what order. Kissing may be a science, may have some elements of strategy, sure, but they're so far outside my wheelhouse that I can't pin any of it down. I might be doing all of this wrong.

"Stop thinking so much." Olivia taps my temple with her index and middle finger and smiles like she knows me. I realize that it's because she does. She really does. "This is good. We're good." She stops for a moment, and a look of what can only be described as fear flashes across her face. "Right? We're good?"

I nod so vigorously it feels like I'm about to separate my head from my body.

"We're good."

When her smile comes back it's easily the best thing I've ever seen. I'm so gone on this girl it would be embarrassing if the way her entire body leans into mine like she can't let go tells me that she's in this just as deep as I am right now.

"Okay," she says. "Good."

I grab my guitar and the open case from where they sit on the ground backstage, and we mutter giggled apologies as we rush past the last remaining contestants and outside. I lean against the side of the barn and pull Olivia to me by her waist and she presses another kiss to my lips. My hat is tilted slightly to the side and I'm sighing like some romance-novel heroine as Olivia straightens it for me. Who even am I?

"Let's go somewhere," she says, her eyes glittering and locked on mine.

"Where are we gonna go?" I ask. But it doesn't matter. I don't care where we go, not really.

I think about the miles and miles that this festival stretches, the way the land unfurls beneath us, seemingly endless. We've done so much this weekend already, covered so much ground. I wonder what else there is to do that we haven't already done. Whatever adventure there is to be had though, I trust that Olivia will find it. She always does.

That's how she found me.

Her hands cup my face. She looks back at the stage door of the barn, checking for I don't know what. I watch her as she does, watch the way her throat works as she swallows and her eyes close for just a second. She takes a deep breath and my heart goes syncopated, the rhythm all out of whack.

When she looks back at me, I want to kiss her again. I don't lean in for a peck right away, but she closes the gap between us, stopping right before she reaches my lips.

"I haven't decided yet." I can feel more than hear her words as she adds, "But we have the rest of the weekend to figure it out."

OLIVIA

SATURDAY AFTERNOON

Toni is a good kisser. Wait, no. Let me be more specific.

Toni is an *incredible* kisser. Like, Olympic-qualifying, should land her a full-ride scholarship to any college, Academy Award–worthy, cinematically incredible kisser. When she pulled back when we were standing backstage, after she kissed me so fast it felt like it might have been an accident, I was sure she wouldn't do it again. It had been so quick, and her face had looked so shocked afterward, I just knew I'd never get to do it again. But I had. I freaking *am*.

We're standing outside the performance barn pressed up against the side, and not making any moves to go inside to meet up with Imani and Peter. We were supposed to go find them after our performance fifteen minutes ago, but. Well. Here we are.

We can't stop. I can't stop. I feel feverish and excited and out-of-control in the best way. Her hands slide up my sides and I can't think. Nothing else matters to me in this moment. It's something more than the temporary relief from restlessness that I used to feel with my other dates. This is something deeper.

This is like running a marathon and finally crossing the finish line. This is like jumping off the ledge and being caught before you hit the bottom.

I don't know what my life's purpose is or anything like that, but I know I want to feel the way that I feel right now for as many days as possible until I can't anymore. This warmth that starts in the pit of my stomach and radiates outward, that tells me I've done something good for someone else, that I've brought someone I care about joy or fulfillment or whatever name you put to it—I don't ever want to let that go.

This can't be a mistake, I think. Nothing that feels like this could be wrong.

Toni leans her forehead against mine, her chest rising and falling quickly. Her hands are on both sides of my neck, so gentle, and I shiver at the feeling. I feel like this isn't even my body right now. No one has ever made me feel like I was going to vibrate right out of my skin unless they held on to me the way that she is. It's scary and thrilling and makes everything I ever thought I knew about desire fly right out the window.

How I felt with every ex is nothing compared to this. That was minor league. This is the majors. The is the Super Bowl of lo—

"I feel crazy," she breathes. She giggles, and it's a little hysterical but a lot relatable. "Do you feel crazy? Is it supposed to feel like this? I've never . . ."

"Me either." I shake my head. It's a complete sentence yet an unformed thought, but everything about me feels unformed right now. I've been unmade by Toni Foster.

"No, I mean . . . I've *never*." Her voice is so quiet, it sounds like a confession.

"You've never . . ."

"Kissed anyone before today," she says, looking down. "That, backstage, that was my first kiss."

If it were physically possible, I would swear that she had just stolen the breath straight out of my lungs. Seriously. My throat feels tight, and it's not a telltale sign of an asthma attack, it's something else entirely. Something somehow scarier, bigger.

I don't know how to tell her that I've had hundreds of kisses, with dozens of people, in the front row at concerts and in the janitors' closet at school next to an old mop and in the back seats of too-small cars. But none of that can compare to this.

That it doesn't matter how much she does or doesn't know, or how much practice she's had with how many girlfriends, because this is it. This is what it should feel like.

That I've been searching and searching and here, with her, is the first time I've ever felt found.

"Okay," I say instead. The words are all caught in my throat. I wind my arms around her waist and press my cheek to her chest. I nod, and hope she understands what I'm saying.

Everything is packed into that word, and I trust her to hear it.

Okay as an admission: *I want you like I've never wanted anyone before.*

Okay as a promise: *I won't hurt you. I'll protect you.*

Okay as a plea: *I don't want to let you go. Please don't let me go.*

And when she pulls my body against hers and presses her nose to the top of my head, I know she gets it. This whole time, I've thought she wasn't a talker, that she struggled to communicate. But maybe she *has* been talking to me. Maybe I just didn't know how to listen until now.

"Yeah," I whisper. "Yeah, okay."

We stand together, just sort of breathing the same air for a minute. Until an all-too-familiar voice jars us out of the moment.

"Hey! Hey, you!" Toni's eyes go comically wide at the sound of Festy Frankie behind us, grabs my hand, and pulls me after her. "Stop! Like, Swiper no swiping!"

We're dashing through the Core like we stole something, which, okay we technically did. People barely even notice the twin expressions on our faces though, or the fact that Frankie is right on our heels. I trust that this looks like some kind of fun game, which is why everyone simply smiles absently in our direction as we duck in between vendor booths and attempt to get lost inside a huge crowd gathering for the Kacey Musgraves show that's getting ready to start.

For someone who supposedly spends most of her summers flocking from festival to festival, laying out in the sun, and taking strategically perfect selfies, Festy Frankie is pretty fast. Her bell-bottom crocheted pants seem to be slowing her down some as they keep getting tangled around her ankles, and that's the only thing that gives me and Toni the chance to break away.

Toni takes her hat off to make herself less conspicuous as we get absorbed by the audience. I thank my almighty stars that I'm short enough to qualify for the kids' meal at Applebee's.

I reach in my fanny pack to grab my inhaler and take a puff. But when I look down and realize Toni's hand is still in mine, I blush. I honest-to-goddess *blush*, at something as simple as holding a girl's hand.

I can count on one hand the times I've done this with other people. With me, most of my dates want to skip past the innocent stuff—the hand-holding, silly board game nights, staying up until three in the morning giggling to each other over the phone and refusing to be the one who hangs up first.

"You think the coast is clear?" Toni looks over her shoulder and peeks around my body, like Festy Frankie has somehow shielded herself behind my super imposing five-four frame. I laugh, and Toni looks down at me, smiling halfway like she realizes how ridiculous she's being. "Wow, she can *move*. I figured all the festivals meant plenty of weed, which would inevitably mean an inability to run long distances."

"A fatal underestimation, Miss Foster." She bumps her

shoulder into mine, looks down at where our hands are still locked together, and pulls hers back to rearrange her hat. It doesn't seem like she's eager to do it though, and that fills me with a warm burst of satisfaction.

We get jostled around a little bit by the crowd and she sighs.

"Sometimes I romanticize how nice it is to be here so much that I forget how gross it can be." She dodges out of the way of someone's raised arm threatening to deliver a hairy pit straight to her face. "You wanna dip out of here and regroup?"

Regrouping, in Toni's estimation, is getting cotton candy to share and refilling our water bottles at the hydration station before finding a spot under a tree to try and catch some shade.

"I want to tell you something," she starts. She takes her hat off to rest on top of her stomach and leans back so her head is resting on my thighs.

I pull off more cotton candy than I need to just so I don't say anything embarrassing. Half of every terrible conversation I've had in my life started with "Can I ask you something?" and the other half with the dreaded "We need to talk." I nod, bracing for impact.

We look at each other, and she reaches out to brush some stray cotton candy off my cheek. The touch is so gentle it's barely there.

She smiles.

"I really like this version of you."

TONI

SATURDAY AFTERNOON

I don't know how long we've been sitting together under this tree, but it doesn't feel important anymore. Time and plans and solitude, all the things I thought were most important to me at the beginning of this weekend, disappeared somewhere between the dance barn and this moment.

Maybe this is what my dad meant when he used to say the music is always with us. Olivia is a melody that has made a song of my universe, and I realize I want to spend a long time trying to figure out all the notes. I don't want to rearrange them, but damn do I want to analyze them. To figure out how to play them and when.

"Penny for your thoughts?" I smile up at her and pluck her sunglasses from her face to slide them onto my own. The big, white, heart-shaped frames look out of place on me I'm sure, but I like wearing something of Olivia's.

"A penny? Have you no respect for the working class? It's a fifteen-dollar minimum for my thoughts, ma'am," she says. I laugh and it feels like I won something. Like I've done something very right to deserve to feel this way.

"You're so right." I eat the last of the cotton candy and grin. "The going rate for the thoughts of teenage girls has been undervalued for too long."

She traces the bridge of my nose with a sticky finger before her face turns serious. "I need to tell you—" She pauses briefly before blurting, "Do you like me?"

She asks me as if it's a question with a yes or no answer. As if *like* is even big enough to wrap its arms around all I feel for her.

I can't hear anything around me, can't make out the sound of the muffled band from a stage across the field. I can't see the people in their fringed bikinis and vintage Farmland T-shirts with lineups from years past milling around waiting for the set to start. All I can see is her. The brown of her eyes that go nearly black after the sun sets. The hard press of her lips against each other when she thinks. The tense line of her shoulders as she gears up for what she thinks I'm going to say.

I don't just *like* her.

I could do this, I tell myself. I could have a good thing, and it would be not simple, but spectacular. Not perfect, yet precious. I'm not ready, not exactly, but my mind will just have to catch up with my heart this time. This time I'm going to choose to leap.

My heart rate is ratcheted up high, but in the best kind of way. I reach forward and grab her hand where it rests on her cutoff-clad thigh. I'm going to say it. Those three words I've been thinking all day but too scared to say.

"Olivia, I—"

But I don't get to tell her. I don't get to apologize for whatever I did to make her question whether or not I was in this all the way, or to make her a promise, or ask her all the things I want to ask her.

An all-too familiar snap rings out, and this time there's no mistaking it for a stage effect. All at once, Olivia's eyes go wide, scared, at the sound of a gunshot. She's yanking me to my feet and we're running. And everyone around us is too. Someone is screaming. It might be Olivia, but I can't tell. My feet are too heavy for my body, and I can't keep up. I'm not sure what's happening, and it's happening so *fast*.

"Toni!" she screams, frantically pulling me behind her, the stampede of people around us threatening to level us both. "*Please, we have to run! You have to go faster!*"

And suddenly, it's not a moment I'm living through—it's a memory. I'm sprinting from a gas station on 56th and Georgetown Road, darting into the street, trying to escape, to find someone to help my dad. I'm breathing too hard. I can't see through my own tears. I'm having a panic attack.

Someone's shoulder slams into mine and I stumble. Olivia's crying in front of me, begging me to stand up.

I think distantly that there might be sirens.

I think that I love her.

I think that means I'm going to lose her.

I'm breathing too hard. I'm slipping away into the moment. I'm feeling the overwhelming sensation of fear that gripped me this morning at the DJ Louddoc set. And I don't know how it happened or where she went, but I lose Olivia in the rush of people around me.

It takes everything in me to focus on the voice in my head from this morning, Olivia repeating soothing words over and over until I came back to her. It's enough to get me moving. I'm carried with the rush of people headed toward the exit, and the only thing I want to do is get back to camp. That has to be where Olivia is headed, where Peter and Imani probably are.

So I run.

OLIVIA

SATURDAY AFTERNOON

When I get back to camp, sweaty and sad and so, so scared, the first thing I do is yell for Toni. I lost her; I can't believe I lost her, it's my fault I lost her. I should have held on tighter, but then I couldn't see, couldn't do anything but move with the current of people, and I couldn't find her. She was right there, I had her hand in mine and everything was good, it was so damn good, we were making it work, everything was fine, and then nothing was fine at all. The entire world around us exploded into madness. I'm screaming myself hoarse, but standing still, like my voice alone is enough to undo all the damage that's happened.

"Olivia, Liv, please." Imani is in front of me, her hands gripping my shoulder. "Liv, you're okay. Stop screaming. You have to stop screaming."

Over her shoulder, Peter stands, looking at his phone like it holds the secrets of the universe. His face is so young and so clearly terrified as he repeats, "My phone isn't working. I can't get a signal. There's no way to get a damn signal!"

I try to breathe, try to follow Imani's soothing voice as she pulls me tight against her. Imani. She's always so solid. Her grip is almost crushing, but it's enough to get the fog in my head to clear. I'm able to gauge my surroundings a little more clearly.

Everyone at their tents and climbing into their cars and looking stressed and frantic. People crying. Farmers throwing their camping gear into the beds of their trucks and the trunks of their cars carelessly, ready to take off.

You think you know chaos—you think Black Friday shopping at Walmart or trying to get the new Xbox on release day is the peak of madness—until you're in the middle of the real thing. Until the people around you are screaming for their friends, asking questions that no one can answer, hoping for the best but preparing for the worst.

"Imani, they're already on the station," Peter says, leaning out the open window of Toni's truck. Imani looks at me and runs a hand over my face quickly before saying, "I'm going to listen to this really quick, okay? Just stay here. I'll be right back. Everything will be fine."

I don't know how long I stand there, dazed and lost, before Peter shouts, "Toni! Jesus Christ, you're okay."

Toni limps toward us, and I don't even think before I run straight to her and wrap my arms around her back. I tuck my face into the space between her neck and shoulder and only then do I allow myself to start crying. I'm so glad she's here, that she's okay, that my letting her go didn't end in something terrible. She's still here.

"I thought I lost you," she whispers. It sounds as fractured as I feel.

"I'm here." There's so much I want to say but can't bring myself to get out right now.

She pulls back and wipes at her eyes.

Peter barrels over and kisses Toni square on the forehead. I step away to give them some space as he throws his arms around her neck and she holds on to him for dear life.

"Don't scare me like that again, dude," Peter says.

Imani hops out of the truck and even she reaches out to squeeze Toni's shoulder. The gratitude that everyone is safe is almost strong enough to feel like a physical thing. Maybe we didn't know one another before this weekend started, but now we're a unit. The Farmland spirit: As long as we're here, we're family.

"They said there's no active shooter." Imani puts on her serious professor voice, the voice she uses when she has to tutor me in calc. She closes her eyes, and when she speaks again, her voice wobbles "A single shot was fired. This isn't another—"

Sandy Hook or Pulse or Charleston or Route 91 Harvest festival or or or

The list goes on. Even a place like this, the first place I've felt free and safe and completely at *home* in the longest time, isn't immune to the fear of guns and what they have the ability to do. Even if it didn't touch us this time, the proximity of what could've just as easily been is hard to shake.

"Yeah," Toni answers quietly. "Lucky."

"What did they say about the rest of the festival?" Peter asks.

Imani says they don't know yet, but we should keep the station on since that's the only way to get information right now, given how clogged the cell towers seem to be. Everyone at the campsites nearest us are complaining about the same thing as they pack up.

None of us moves. We just stand in a circle, close to one another, silently.

"I think we need to leave," Imani says. She directs it at me. "It doesn't really matter what they do next, I don't think there's any reason to stay at this point. The festival is over."

What she's saying makes sense. The thought of that though? The idea of leaving here and not knowing what could have been with me and Toni or Imani and Peter or even with the scavenger hunt feels unimaginable. Like taking the key out of the ignition before you've even stopped the car. I'm not ready to go. I'm not ready for the real world. I'm just not ready.

Though there are plenty of people packing up, there are a lot of people staying exactly where they are. There are just as many cars filing out of the campsite right now as there are that remain parked. Some Farmers are still shaken, despite the reality that things aren't as dire as we initially thought, but they're not going anywhere yet. We need to be the ones who stay. At least until the morning.

"We're in no condition to drive back to Indianapolis tonight," I say. I hold my hands out in front of me, palms up, for emphasis. They're still shaking. "We should at least stay until morning."

Imani bites her lip and looks toward our campsite in the distance. I know she wants to say no. I know her rationale is winning out, but I can't go. I just can't.

"We're gonna stay too," Peter says, his voice serious. He looks to Toni and she nods her head in agreement. "We should be safe for now."

Nothing is safe, I want to say. I think of all the people I've felt safe with before who turned out to be unsafe in their own ways. The places I've gone that I expected to be a refuge that only turned out to make things impossibly worse. But there's something soothing about the idea of staying together tonight, the four of us riding out the storm. Maybe not safe, exactly, but closer to it together.

Imani sighs.

"Fine," she says. "For tonight."

I chance a look at Toni, and her eyes are right on me. I want to reach across the circle that we've created and make a home inside the circle of her arms instead, but I don't. Not yet anyway. Because whether I'm holding on to her or not, that look counts for something.

I think it might count for everything.

TONI

SATURDAY EVENING

The four of us sit together at Olivia's and Imani's campsite all night. We listen to the Farmland radio station, waiting for more updates, and light a fire in the grill we brought along.

Everyone is coping differently; between chancing looks at Olivia like she's afraid she'll disappear if she takes her eyes off her, Imani has been checking her phone religiously, trying for a decent enough signal to get some more information from major news outlets about what's happened. Olivia sits in the chair near me, legs tucked underneath herself and a blanket wrapped around her shoulders. I'm plucking at the strings of my guitar, trying to find a melody that will pull us all out of this space for a second.

But it's Peter whose reaction scares me the most. My best friend, who usually has no shortage of smiles or positive anecdotes, sits silently off to the side.

"This is crazy," he mutters. It's just gotten dark, and still no one knows anything new. The Farmers at the campsite next to us packed up in a hurry an hour ago, leaving nothing but a stray bottle of some locally brewed beer behind. He looks around at the three of us and repeats, louder, "This is crazy. I wanna know who did this."

He pushes himself off the ground and runs a hand through his hair. He took it out of his bun earlier and hasn't pulled it back again. He looks frazzled, the curls sticking up in every direction with how often he's pulled at them tonight. He even switched out of his crop top and put on an old black hooded sweatshirt. When I catch his eyes over the fire, I realize he doesn't even look scared. He looks furious.

"Are we really just going to sit here and let this go? We should be doing something." He clenches his hands into fists at his side. He paces back and forth. "You know, Andrew Jackson never backed down from anything. He was in over one hundred duels. That's—"

"Oh my God, would you give it a rest, Peter?" Imani snaps. "Enough with the presidents, for the love of God. Dead white slave owners aren't going to help us right now." She stands and throws her hands up. "We don't know *anything*. Don't you get that? We have no facts. There's nothing we can do."

"Some of us aren't built like robots, Imani!" Peter's voice is angrier than I've ever heard it, and the sound of it makes me flinch. "Some of us care about action. Some of us are able to make decisions based on *feelings*, not facts."

Imani sucks in a breath, and for the first time all weekend, I see her face betray how she feels. Instead of snapping back though, she retreats into herself. She sits down next to Olivia and the two lean against each other for support. Peter turns his back on the circle, on the fire, and closes his eyes. His comment was way out of line. The Peter I know doesn't snap at people, especially not like this, accusations laced with innuendo and ire.

"You need to relax, okay?" I set my guitar down and move to stand beside him. I run my hands over my face and lower my voice so only he can hear me. "Imani is right. We leave or we wait it out. Those are our options."

I understand his frustration, I can feel it too, gripping and twisting at me. How dare someone take this place from us? This weekend? All evening, all I've done is replay the moment after the gunshot earlier. Every bone in my body was attuned to Olivia. All my thoughts oriented toward her safety. *What if I lose her? What if she doesn't run fast enough? Why did I decide to let another person into my heart when that only ever leads to more pain?*

Peter nods but doesn't sit back down. He breathes out once, slowly.

"I'm gonna call it an early night," he says, his voice flat. He doesn't seem to be speaking to anyone in particular. He doesn't make eye contact as he grabs his A's cap off the grass and silently marches back to our tent. "See you in the morning."

After that, it feels like there's nothing left to do but call it a night. Eventually, the fire flickers out, and everyone drifts off to their tents, all of us tired by the events of the day and preparing for tomorrow. Maybe we'll be leaving in the morning, maybe Kittredge will still perform tomorrow night. Maybe this is the last Farmland we'll ever have. Nothing is certain.

But as I change into my pajamas and climb into my sleeping bag on an air mattress next to an already-snoring Peter, I know one thing for sure: I don't think I'm strong enough for this.

For a life that leads me toward the music, for falling in love with Olivia—for any of it.

I lay there in silence for an hour, long after the last voices of people around me quiet to nothing. Until the zipper on our tent goes up, and I sit up quickly to squint at the intruder in the low light. Olivia's braids are pulled into a low bun and wrapped up in a leopard-print silk scarf. Her face is completely makeup free as she pokes her head inside. She doesn't say anything, just waves me out.

Peter is snoring steadily beside me, so I grab my shoes and go without a second thought.

The air has a chill, but it's not exactly cold. I pull on an old flannel before I follow Olivia away from my tent, just in case. She doesn't speak right away and neither do I. What is there to say when you feel like the foundation of your world has been shaken?

There is no balm to make it better, no magical phrase I can offer that would provide either of us any comfort. So I just walk.

Our arms brush against each other enough times that eventually we link our pinkies together and allow our hands to swing between us. There's something about it that feels more intimate than holding hands. The thought of it makes me want to cry.

The festival is mostly asleep. All the acts that were scheduled to go on this evening were canceled as the organizers decide what to do next. Even though we know it wasn't an attack, all of Farmland feels like it's shifted on its axis. Right now, the all-night party in the dance barn should be raging on, the bass loud enough to be heard from just about anywhere in the campground. The lights from the rides in the Core should be shining so bright we'd barely be able to see the stars.

We should be doing the Farmer wave to everyone who passes us as we walk down the gravel path, but instead there's nothing—no one, barring the occasional person walking to or from the port-o-potty bank. All I can hear is Olivia's small puffs of breath and the sound of our shoes as they crunch along the walk.

"Olivia," I finally say after we've been walking for about fifteen minutes with no end in sight. "Where are we going?"

She stops and places her hands on both of my cheeks. I expect her to kiss me but she doesn't.

"If this is the last night of Farmland . . ." she says. Her voice is low and serious and I hate it. I hate what's happened here and that this girl in front of me—this girl who has the best smile, who should always be smiling—is urging me to cling to what's left of this with her. We shouldn't have to cling. "I don't want to waste it."

She says she wants to go to the Farmland sign to take a picture, a rite of passage for any first-time Farmer, just in case she doesn't get a chance to do it tomorrow. Or, today, technically, since it's already after midnight. But once we get to the gates that would normally take us inside the Core, there are barricades in front of them. And a sign that says NO ENTRY UNTIL FURTHER NOTICE.

"Shit." Olivia's voice is a whisper, even though there's no one around to hear us, and not that anyone would care if they did. She finds a gap in the barricades near where they meet the fence and slips between them and into the Core. I look around for any lingering security before I do the same.

Once we're inside, we head straight to the sign. Everything inside the Core has been powered down for the night, something I've never seen at Farmland. Even the sign, in all its legendary glowing glory, is off—its big, gleaming bulbs at rest. She stops to snap a photo of it—the flash briefly disorienting in the low light—but doesn't seem to want to be in it anymore. I don't ask what changed her mind.

She keeps walking until we're at the Ferris wheel. It's also powered down, ghost-like, but in for a penny, in for a pound, Olivia jumps the low barricade that blocks the entrance.

She settles into the bench of the rocking gondola and pulls her knees up to her chest. She's dressed in nothing but her sleep shorts and an oversized T-shirt, so I pull off my flannel and drape it over her shoulders when she shivers a little. She pulls it tight around her body as I sit down next to her.

"Should be more security," I say. Short, emotionless, easier than what I really want to say.

She nods and leans her head against my shoulder. We haven't had any quiet moments between us since we met—not slow, honest-to-God quiet moments like these—and part of me wants to sit with this stillness for a long time. This space where it's just the two of us, no distractions, while the air around us vibrates with an electricity only we create. But I know it's fleeting. This moment, like everything, will be here and gone.

"I'm sort of an old pro of getting into situations I'm not supposed to be in." She laughs, but it's sad.

We rock back and forth in the gondola for a second, and I let myself imagine a normal night at Farmland, being three hundred feet above it all, looking down on the neon madness below next to a girl I like so much it scares me. A girl I like so much I was willing to forget my own cardinal rule. A girl I'm already sharpening myself against because this can't last. I can't—I won't be hurt by losing someone I love again.

But I decide to let myself have this moment. This snapshot.

"Toni?"

"Yeah?"

"I have to tell you something."

OLIVIA

SATURDAY NIGHT

Toni doesn't rush me to say anything when she realizes I'm struggling to speak. I don't look at her as I try to figure out the words to allow her to see into the worst of me.

The problem with being the type of person who is good at falling in love is the fact that eventually people catch on to it—especially in a school as small as Park Meade. They see a revolving door of boyfriends and girlfriends and start to make assumptions about what that means about you. Or what it means you'll be willing to do, I guess.

I didn't know that when Troy asked me out though. I didn't understand until it was too late.

We'd been together for a grand total of two weeks before he leaned up against my locker after third period and tugged at my uniform tie so that I was standing close enough for him to whisper over the sound of our classmates rushing around us and shouting at one another down the hallways.

"You should come over to my place tonight," he said, lips brushing against my temple. There are rules at Park Meade against public displays of affection, but I didn't mind. It felt good, and bold, that Troy would so blatantly disregard the rules to be close to me. "After the football game."

Troy's house was almost always the spot for parties on Friday nights in the off-season. I'd never needed a formal invitation before, not even when we weren't dating. He was the epitome of the high school heartthrob stereotype: handsome, a little dumb, a sense of humor that was meaner than it was funny, and absolutely, unbelievably good at basketball. He'd been on every all-star team and "players to watch" list since middle school and had gotten the school its first 2A State Championship last year.

Basketball wasn't invented in Indiana, but some still call it the birthplace of the game. *Hoosiers* didn't become one of the most popular sports movies of all time because it was such a riot to watch. People love it because it's true. (Seriously, to so much as talk about IU men's basketball's Christian Watford making the buzzer-beating shot against number-one-ranked University of Kentucky in 2011 still brings some alums to tears.)

To be a small-town basketball star in Indiana, especially one on your way to the league, makes you bigger than a celebrity. It makes you untouchable.

"Of course I'll be there!" I giggled. "Imani will have to drive me, obviously, which means I have to wait for her to finish her homework because you know she won't go into the weekend with an unfinished—"

"No, I mean just you. I've got the place to myself for the night." He brushed his brown-blond hair to the right so it wasn't hanging down in his eyes. "I think we should be alone."

The way he said *be alone* told me everything I needed to know. He'd been getting more and more insistent about the fact that we should be moving faster than we were since the day after he asked me out. I knew what he wanted, what he thought I was already well-experienced with, but I was too embarrassed to tell him the truth. That no matter how many people I'd dated and been dumped by, I'd never had sex with any of them.

Maybe it hadn't felt right or been the right person or they hadn't stuck around long enough for us to get there, but whatever the reason, I wasn't the person Troy thought I was. And it was a constant reminder that another person in my life wanted something that—try as I might—I couldn't give them.

"Oh," I said. I stepped back slightly and shut my locker with a soft click. "Troy, I . . . I can't really do *that* tonight."

I could see myself, even then, and knew what a cliché I had become: the delicate little flower of a girlfriend afraid to give her virginity away to the hot jock. But I also knew that I liked being the girl under his arm, liked being the person who people envied for once. I liked that Kayla Mitchell—the captain of the girls' tennis team and junior homecoming queen—told everyone that Troy would never settle down if not with her, just for him to ask me out a week later.

It made me feel powerful, *valuable*.

"Well, what are we gonna do, babe? I'm a growing boy, I need something to keep me from going crazy." He growled then, like it was all some big joke, and so I laughed a little like I thought it was funny. Because that was the role I played.

If he was the Hot Jock, then I was the Doting Girlfriend. I dropped by his locker in the morning with notes from classes I knew he wasn't paying attention to. I showed up after his practices with freshly baked cookies or a bag of takeout from Steak 'n Shake and offered myself up to him like a prize he'd already won. I'd kiss him at his car, to the soundtrack of his teammates jeering, and I'd slip into the passenger seat and let him drive me home. I molded myself perfectly into the character I needed to be to keep him. Except for that one thing.

But I knew the underlying truth of it all: If he didn't get it from me, he'd find it somewhere else.

Making the decision to send him pictures of me in front of my floor-length mirror at home later that night, dressed in nothing more than the only sexy-ish bra and panty set I owned, didn't take that long. I'd like to say that I wrestled with the idea for a while, tried to come up with a pros and cons list and found that the reward outweighed the risk, but that's not true. That's not me.

I don't think ahead, I don't consider consequences. I just leap and hope that the fall is worth it.

So when he sent me back the tongue emojis in lieu of any real response, I still felt like I'd done the right thing. It wasn't until Imani called me at one a.m., half-frantic, that I knew I'd finally gone too far. This time, I'd leapt straight off the cliff and there was nothing below to save me.

And I was paying the price.

The pictures made it to Confidential, and on Monday, they were plastered all over my locker. The entire school had seen me practically naked, and there was nothing that could've prepared me for how exposed that would make me feel. It's different being bold and noticeable when you choose it, I learned, but when that choice is taken away from you, it's like being stripped bare in the worst way possible.

The fallout happened pretty quickly after that: Troy's very public denial that he had anything to do with the photos being leaked. His insistence that I released the pictures myself for attention. The embarrassing and unceremonial breakup. Principal Meyer delaying and then delaying again the judicial hearing to come to a decision about what to do about Troy's involvement in the photos getting out, or whether he was involved at all, until after basketball season. My mom not speaking to me. Nia practically disowning me. The friends that I thought I had shunning me for having the audacity to try and hold Troy accountable instead of just living with what I'd done.

I had my best friend, but I didn't have much else. I wanted to go back on it all, to say that it was no big deal, that I didn't want to move forward with any punishment, but I couldn't bring myself to do it. Every time I almost marched myself down to the principal's office to ask them what they were going to do, remembering Troy's giddy face doing a post-game interview on WTHR after another win would stop me.

There are no good options for someone like me. If I testify against him, I could destroy his future. I could position him to lose his basketball scholarships and his only chance to play division one basketball. I'd make my mom's work life so uncomfortable that she might have to leave her dream job. I would become even more of an outcast at school, and the worst kind.

I would never get those pictures back anyway. I would never get that sense of privacy back. I would just be making things harder for everyone. People like Troy don't get punished, they get full rides to college. They get the glory and the sympathy and a line of people who will always call them heroes.

People like me, on the other hand? People like me are lucky if we end up with anything at all.

There will be a hearing at the end of the week, and Troy Murphy will be there in his crisp white button-down and that bright red tie he always used to wear on game days. He will smile and he will charm and he will walk away unscathed. Because I won't be there to defend myself. I refuse to beg them to care, to explain to them how I was hurt and all the things I lost. No, my silence is the only way for me to hold on to what's left of my dignity.

He's already taken everything else.

TONI

SATURDAY NIGHT

The more Olivia says, the more my heart breaks. I want to go back in time and destroy all the people who have ever hurt her. I want to find this boy and use more than just my words to tell him that Olivia's body, and her privacy, will always, *always* matter more than his ability to dribble a basketball. I want so much more for her than what she's been given.

But all I have right now are my words, and that's never been my strong suit.

Once, when I was younger, I'd been crying in my room at night, missing my dad. My mom cracked open the door and padded across the wood floor to sit next to me on my bed. She shushed me quietly and placed a soft hand on my back, rubbing it in circles before saying, "Sometimes people don't know how to show you how much they love you." I hiccupped into my pillow. "But that doesn't mean they don't."

It was the first time my mom and I had ever acknowledged the Jackson Foster–sized hole that existed in our house, in our family. And it didn't seem fair. I wondered how many times she'd said the same thing to herself, after a missed phone call or another tour extension. I wondered if she felt the same way that I did: like no amount of goodness would be enough to make someone want to stay.

Olivia sniffles and pulls herself closer to me, like she could hide herself from everything bad that's ever happened to her in my arms. And I finally understand where my mom went wrong. Loving someone is being big enough to admit when you mess up, and then doing everything in your power not to do it again.

"If someone loves you, they should show you. And if they don't know how, loving someone means you learn," I say. "You deserve to be handled with care, Olivia. I don't know what those people . . ."

My voice hardens before I stop to gather my thoughts. The thought of all those exes, of what Troy did to her, makes my entire body pull taut. I've never fought anyone before, but in that moment I'm sure I could rip him apart with my bare hands.

"That big love you give everyone else—you deserve to save some for yourself. You're worth that much. You're worth every good thing."

"I've dated so many people." She wipes at her eyes with the back of her hand. "And it always ends up the same. A disaster. I'm the problem."

"There's nothing wrong with wanting people to love you. Lots of people, even. That's your right."

"Yeah but . . . it's always wrong. It always ends up ruined. It's me. It's what I do," she says, eyes shutting tight.

"Look, you're not a bad person for wanting someone to love you. That's not wrong, okay?" I pull back slightly. I tilt her chin up so she has to look me in my eyes. "Okay, Olivia? They were wrong for treating you poorly. You have to know that."

"But I *should've* known better. I—" She pushes up and shakes her head. "I always do this. You don't know, because you haven't seen all of me yet, but I always go too far. It's just inside me." She holds her hand in front of her chest. "Something in here keeps me from being like other people. Logic, reason, all fly out the window when I . . ." she pauses.

I don't wait for her to finish her thought. I need her to understand.

"Love is showing up. Period. You deserve someone who shows up."

I know it's true. I can feel the truth of it as deeply as I've felt anything. But that's the problem. If love means showing up, being better to the people you care about than my dad was to me and my mom, then I'm not sure I'm capable of it.

And I'm not sure I'll ever be the type of person who is.

FARMLAND
MUSIC AND ARTS FESTIVAL
SUNDAY

"You're asking us a question about being in love, but, you know, I don't think that's what the music has ever been about. Our songs are the before and after. The climb and the fall. That's the scary part."

–Teela Conrad from the Kittredge *Rolling Stone* cover story, January 2019

OLIVIA

SUNDAY MORNING

I don't remember falling asleep with Toni in the Ferris wheel, but I wish I did. Because then I could stay in the moment of feeling safe and protected in her arms as we tangled up in the too-small seat a little bit longer. Instead, I'm being woken up by a burly security guy—with eyebrows that are surprisingly immaculately arched—roughly shaking my shoulder.

"You two can't be here," he says. "Y'all shouldn't have even been able to get in."

I'm disoriented for a second until Toni's arms drop from where they've been holding me and she mumbles, "Could use some better bedside manner."

The security guard stands watch with an unamused expression until we get out of the gondola, and when I look over my shoulder at him he's shaking his head at the two of us. But it's not the type of headshake of an annoyed employee, it's the headshake of someone who gets it—why two girls might risk a breaking and entering charge for one last night together—but has to do his job anyway. Or at least that's what I tell myself.

I expect Toni to grab my hand on the walk back, but she doesn't. There's a foot of space between us that I don't understand, but I try not to read too far into it. I try to hold on to the buzz of knowing I spent the night wrapped up in her arms, even if it's the last time we get to do it for a while. I try to hold on to the fact that she knows everything about me, that I told her the entire story of me and Troy and the damage I cause just by being me, and she didn't leave. She looked at me with so much patience it hurt, and she held me anyway.

No one has ever done that for me before—not even Imani. No judgment, no *I told you so*, no disappointed looks. Just held me close, without the intention of holding me together. Like she trusted I was strong enough to make it through without her, but she wanted to be there for me anyway.

We haven't talked about it, but this must be the real deal. This must be what it feels like to be with someone and know—really know, deep in your bones—that it isn't going to be some short-lived thing. That you're in it for the long haul. When I look over at Toni, lines from where her sleeve pressed against her face in the night and yawning without even thinking to cover her mouth, I don't see this ending tomorrow. I see more mornings waking up together in her dorm room in Bloomington or weekends watching shows at The Vogue or nights debating the best songs in Fleetwood Mac's discography.

Whole years of possibilities stretch in front of me.

"I'm gonna . . ." Once we reach our pod of campsites, she jerks her thumb in the direction of her and Peter's spot. I want to kiss her, but I figure maybe with morning breath it's not the best move for either of us. I nod.

"Okay, um, see you later."

When I turn my back, I'm a little delirious, and more than a little nervous at the thought of what last night must have meant. I was honest with Toni, and she still stayed with me. That has to mean something, right?

"Where were you all night?" Imani demands as soon as I get within reach. I look around our campsite and everything that was inside the tent is now out in the grass, and she's started breaking down the tent. I immediately feel my heartbeat pick up, a sign of my body entering panic mode.

It's too early for this. We're not supposed to be leaving yet. We can't. *I* can't.

After my conversation with Toni last night, I feel like there's so much left to do. So much left to figure out. It took sitting with her, crying on her, being honest with her to see what kept getting swallowed up by the trolls on Confidential and the unsubtle warnings from my mother and the pitying looks from Imani all these months. Maybe I am a little much. Maybe I am a little over-the-top, but that doesn't mean I don't deserve to be treated with dignity.

Troy discarding me, violating my privacy, and then moving on to the next girl with no punishment or accountability isn't on me—that's on him. So the consequences should be his to bear as well.

I wasn't sure about testifying against him before—didn't think it would be worth any good—but if only for me, if only because I deserve better, I think I have to. No matter what comes after. If Imani would just listen to me, she'd be happy I figured things out. But she fumes instead.

"I've been texting and calling since I woke up and you weren't here." Imani shakes her phone at me. I shake my head, disagreeing before she's said anything else.

"Why are you packing everything up?" I start reaching for things she's already packed to move them back to where they belong. The couple who used to be on our left is already gone and the group of friends who were camping to our right are shoving their stuff into the back of their SUV. "We don't even know if they're canceling things today. We can't just leave."

Imani rolls her eyes. "Yeah, well, I'm ready to go. I think I've had about enough adventure for one weekend." She turns back to the tent and starts folding the obnoxiously colored nylon. "Why didn't you take your phone? I was worried about you."

"I didn't even think about it," I say. I want to get her to stop but

I don't know how. Imani is a woman on a mission, and she's ready to go. "Imani, wait—"

"You were with Toni all night, weren't you?" Her voice isn't loud, or angry, just toneless.

I know the promise I made Imani, that this would be a best friend weekend, but that was before. She spent the past two days getting closer to Peter, laying the groundwork for what could be something really great (thanks to me!), and I now have Toni. Imani didn't want me to bail, to leave her by herself out here while I chased after the high of being wanted by somebody. But this wasn't that.

I wasn't chasing Toni. I stumbled into her, almost literally, and she caught me. And has kept catching me all weekend.

"Yes," I say carefully. "But it's good! I told her everything, and she was okay with it. She's . . . different."

She breathes out slowly. "What about our best friend weekend, Olivia?"

If she would just listen, she would see that the change to our weekend was a good thing. The best thing. I open my mouth to tell her I changed my mind about testifying against Troy, that I'm going to do it. That Toni helped me see what I hadn't been able to see before, but she cuts me off.

"You haven't thought about that, but I bet you figured out exactly what the color scheme for you and Toni's wedding is going to be. Or no, I know, you've probably already decided to name your kids after some pretentious dead musicians!" She runs a hand over her hair, the loose wave of it still somehow flawless after a weekend in this humidity. "This is your problem, Olivia. You're always worried about the wrong people."

And wow. That one hurts. It's confirmation of exactly what I've feared this entire time, that Imani sees me the same way everyone else in my life sees me: as a hopeless screwup. That my judgment can't be trusted anymore. That maybe it never could.

"That's not fair. You haven't even given her a chance. How would you know she's the wrong person?"

"Because you're the one who chose her."

I gasp. I don't mean to, but it's like she's poked a hole in me and I'm deflating where I stand. Neither of us speaks. We just stare at each other, waiting for the other to break. Finally, Imani sighs.

"I'm going to see if I can find some food," she says. She turns away from me to grab her fanny pack. "When I get back, I'm leaving. I can't wait to get as far away from this festival and this nightmare of a weekend as possible." She looks over her shoulder. "You have a half hour. You can either come with me or stay here, but I'm gone."

She walks off in the direction of the Core, and I fall back into a chair that she hasn't packed up yet.

Imani would never leave without me, so I know her threat is empty. But the fact that she would even say it, that she would even throw it out there, makes me pause. Is she really that annoyed with me? Is she really that jealous because of this misplaced belief that she's been demoted by Toni somehow? Have we really grown apart that much?

TONI

SUNDAY MORNING

I grab my guitar out of the case and sit on top of the cooler. I think about playing here with Olivia the other night, about how much clarity the act of being back in touch with the music gave me. Maybe it'll unveil another kind of Truth to me. I try to strum some of the chords to "The Argonauts," but there's no finesse. No magic. The notes are right, but everything feels stilted, mechanical. It's like it was eight months ago all over again, and I hate it.

I try again. And again. And the results are all the same. I'm frustrated at myself and my acoustic and this stupid festival and I can't do it. I can't do any of this.

Peter is still sleeping, or at least I think he must be. He hasn't crawled out of the tent, and that's usually a pretty sure sign that he isn't yet in the land of the living. I'm glad to be alone for a second, even in my anger.

For just a moment before performing yesterday, I had such clarity about my life, but none of it had to do with a career. It had to do with a feeling, and that feeling had everything to do with Olivia. But last night as Olivia was telling me about her ex, I felt the niggling sensation in the back of my head that I've felt so many times before. The voice that whispers not to go any further, not to get any closer. Because if we do, one of us was going to end up broken by the other.

Because that's just what happens when you care too much: You shatter and shatter until there's nothing left of your pieces but dust.

I've been trying to recapture the feeling from our kiss and from that electric moment on stage ever since they happened, and they're all-consuming—flames licking up my skin and burning everything in their wake. I can feel it already, the insatiability that my dad must have felt all the time. To want something so much that it eclipses all else. I came here to find a plan for my life, something that could make my mom proud and give me purpose. But for a few hours as I was tangled up in Olivia, I forgot that. And that's dangerous.

Neither of us needs more danger in our lives. We need a love more stable than what we're used to. And that's when I know. I only have one choice, and it's going to hurt like hell.

When Olivia walks over, her braids down and swinging behind her as she moves, I tap into the old Toni. Ardsley Academy Toni, the queen of the North Pole. It takes all my energy not to launch myself at her, kiss her, and tell her that I'm sorry. That I wish I had a better solution than this. But there isn't one. I don't want to hurt her, so I have to let her go.

She looks like I feel, a type of urgency on her face I've never seen before. I set my guitar back into the case and stand up to meet her. She immediately wraps her arms around my waist, and I pull her closer to me even though I know I shouldn't.

"Toni." She says my name like a prayer, softly, reverently. A balloon inflates in my chest and I can barely breathe. I want to keep holding her, forever maybe. She leans her forehead against my shoulder. "I'm so glad I have you."

I convince myself that it's not just for my sake. That this is good for her in the long run too. She doesn't know, really, the kind of person I am. The kind who goes cold on a dime and doesn't share her feelings and holds people at arm's length. She doesn't know what's in my very DNA—that I am the spitting image of a man who chose the music over the people he loved at every turn, that given the chance one day I might do the very same thing.

I place my hands on her shoulders and hold her away from me. When she looks at me I see everything in those eyes. Every possible future. Every inevitable heartbreak.

I see my mom pretending not to cry on anniversaries spent alone. I see pictures of me at piano recitals with only one smiling parent instead of two. I see my dad, sweeping into town and charming us into forgetting how long he'd been away and how soon he intended to leave. I see myself starting college in a few days, and being the adult my dad never was.

I'm going to choose the safe thing, the stable thing, like I was always supposed to. "Olivia," I say. "We need to talk."

OLIVIA

SUNDAY MORNING

Anyone who's ever said all heartbreak is created equal has clearly never had their heart broken by Toni Foster.

A coldness hits me like a wave as I walk away from her campsite, goose bumps covering my arms even though it's warmer already than it was yesterday. I'm shaking, my arms wrapped around myself barely enough to keep my entire body from coming apart at the seams. I text Imani that I need her—that Toni and me are done—the same way I always do. Just like the script lays out. But I'm met with radio silence on the other end. I wander back to my nonexistent campsite in a daze, not even in tears. I think I'm in disbelief.

How is it that one person can be so massively wrong so consistently? What is it about me that's wired incorrectly? That makes my judgment so bad and my love so easy to reject?

It's always me who drives people away. It's always something I've done or said. It doesn't matter whether I'm myself from the beginning, or playing a character—this is how it'll always end up for me. This is who I am.

A familiar restlessness bubbles up inside me. An urgency to run and go and *do*.

I'll never be like Nia with her perfect relationship and grades and looks. I'll never be the kind of girl who people look at and think, *Wow, she's really got it all together, huh?* Some people are the ones who get left, and some people are the ones who do the leaving. There's no question about which side of the equation I fall on now, if there ever was before.

I run my hands over my face haphazardly, I straighten my back. I know what character I have to play to fix this.

The first thing I do is take a much-needed shower.

I'm covered in a layer of grime from two days of sweat and dirt. Not even another morning using those handy bath wipes the message board suggested is enough to get it off. I grab my flip-flops, towels, and soap and walk to the bank of showers. I slip some quarters in the shower to activate the water before slipping inside. I take extra care scrubbing every bit of dust from my skin. I rub my arms until they're practically raw. I settle into the ritual of washing away the pieces of myself that I'll no longer hold on to.

It's what I did with Troy, with Aaron, Jessie, Kai—the list goes on. As I wash, I try to feel relief at the thought of the person I've been this weekend circling the drain, but all I can summon up is a deep, buzzing tension like a rubber band getting ready to snap. I know this feeling though. I greet it like an old frenemy. I want it gone, but I crave its familiarity. At least when I metamorphize like this, I know exactly what to expect. I know what I have to lose in order to gain what I want.

That's where I screwed up with Toni, I think. I was in uncharted territory. I lost my footing. I slipped up, but didn't even know I was slipping. It won't happen again.

I stay in the shower until the water runs cold and then I stay a little longer. I shut off the water and the way the towel rubs against my freshly scrubbed skin chafes. I march back to camp and pull on my outfit in the back seat of the car. I spend an inordinately long time putting on makeup in the rearview mirror. I'll wear this uniform like armor.

I'll apologize to Toni. I don't know what I'd be apologizing for, exactly, but it's not like I haven't done it before. I can say sorry for whatever I did to make her run this morning. I can retreat a little, I can become a little different, box up the parts of myself that made things too much for her to handle.

I can't be fixed, but I can fix *this*.

I don't want to feel this way anymore. I brace myself. I slip into a new skin.

I walk over to Peter's and Toni's camp.

"Olivia." Peter is leaning against the truck when I arrive. His hair is wet and disheveled like he's just gotten done with a shower of his own, but he's dressed in his usual: dirty black Vans, what used to be skinny jeans cut into jorts, and a cropped blue-and-green tie-dye Bowie T-shirt. "Toni's not here."

My heart drops. Of course Toni wouldn't still be here. She's probably in the Core already, going about her life. Peter should be with her though. I notice his voice lacks its usual glowing enthusiasm.

"What's going on?" I ask, trying to keep my voice neutral.

He holds up the phone in his hand and shakes it. "Imani's pretty pissed with the way I acted last night. Texted me, said you guys were leaving and that I shouldn't reach out again . . . You know how it goes." He slides down the side of the truck and lands in a heap in the grass. He looks up at me with a frown. "I overheard you and T this morning, by the way. I'm sorry."

I take that as a sign to sit down next to him. If I hadn't been dumped on a moving float in front of all the sophomore class officers during the homecoming parade once, the fact that I was broken up with in hearing distance of another person would probably embarrass me more. But I must be at the stage of breakup grief where I skyrocket straight past humiliation, because all I can say is:

"I came to get her back."

Peter huffs. He looks down at his phone but doesn't say anything for a long time.

"Sometimes the best thing you can give someone is their space, you know?" he says, shrugging. "Goodbye can be the right answer, even if it doesn't feel like it."

Peter, who knows her better than anyone, says it's over.

My chest tightens in the worst, most familiar way. I know what it sounds like to be told to give up. To be told that it's never gonna happen, it's time to move on, that I wasn't good enough in the first place. I want to run. I want to do something reckless. I want to chase away this feeling.

I clench and unclench my fists, trying to ground myself. I try to slow my thoughts, but I can't. They're racing. Everything is moving too quick.

Peter runs his hands through his hair again. It's a nervous habit, I know, but I think absently how it makes him look like Twitter's crush of the month. Peter with his wide smile and puppy-dog eyes and heart on his sleeve. He's . . . cute. I run through a checklist of Peter's qualities without even meaning to. He's smart—smart enough to keep up with Imani, even. Funny. Nice. And above all, he's transparent.

There's no guessing game with Peter. You know where you stand with him at all times. If he wants you, you'll know it—you'll become the sun in his solar system.

All at once, my spine straightens. My vision feels sharper, renewed. This is familiar too. More familiar, even, than the rejection. It comes over me so quickly I almost don't realize what's happening.

"So, Peter," I start, laying a hand gently on his forearm where it rests in his lap. My voice pitches higher, just slightly, just enough. "Remind me. What did you say was the problem with Odd One's live performance yesterday?"

He brightens immediately. His eyes light up as they lock on mine. He's enthusiastic, and where there's enthusiasm, there's pliability.

I don't know how long we sit next to each other, talking about these things I don't care about, but I allow myself to fall into it. I allow it to wash over me. Every time he laughs at something I say or looks at me while I'm speaking without breaking eye contact, I get that same thrill I used to get when I locked into a new target. The knot in my chest begins to loosen.

Peter's arm is pressed against mine as we lean against the side of the truck, and I can feel the way the sun has warmed his skin. He rumbles with laughter at some joke I barely realize I'm making and bumps his shoulder into mine on purpose. I remember him saying that pop punk is his favorite genre, so I dig up everything I know about it.

I reference basement shows I've seen of up-and-coming pop punk artists in the Midwest. I mention a fact I gleaned from an old essay on Fall Out Boy about how they sold out after their third album, but I say it with such authority I know it makes me sound like I really care. Like I've listened to them faithfully for years, even though I couldn't tell you the name of any song of theirs besides "Dance, Dance," and that's only because people used it in a dance challenge on Confidential last year.

Sitting next to Peter—weaving this narrative of Olivia Brooks as a Pop Punk Princess for him—is like picking up an instrument after a little while away. All it takes is a few minutes of practice and I'm playing like a pro again.

This is good, I tell myself. This is nice. Peter is a good guy. I don't know why Imani didn't jump on her chance with him this weekend. Peter is funny and smart and handsome and harmless. He's great.

He's the type of person I should be with. I've spent all weekend with Toni, when maybe this is what I should've been doing instead. Peter wouldn't dump me after I bared my ugly past to him, even though he said I deserved better than that. Peter wouldn't push me away because it'd be too much trouble to know me after this festival was over.

I've found a soft place to land.

TONI

SUNDAY MORNING

If I think about the way Olivia's face looked when I told her I couldn't do this anymore, I'm positive I'll fall apart. I try to shut it down. I do what I've always done—I welcome the numbness that comes with being alone in the moments I most wish I weren't.

I decide to take a walk. I don't know where I'm going or how long I have to walk around before we get word about what's going to happen next—whether the festival shuts down completely or they try to salvage the pieces that are left—so I decide to just go. As I move through the campgrounds, I'm hit with the strongest wave of nostalgia I've ever felt.

No matter what happens from here, this place will never be

245

the same. The lit-up totems with the heads of their favorite TV characters on top, the campsites that are decked out like five-star resorts, the space in front of the stage where I sat on my dad's shoulders for the first time to watch a concert—there's no coming back from this. There will likely be another Farmland next year, of course, but this place will never feel quite the same as it used to. Farmland is the place where I thought I might lose my life, and the place where I did lose Olivia.

What was once a place of safety and comfort separate from the world isn't anymore. Probably wasn't ever, honestly. But now it's impossible to ignore.

Once I get closer to the Core, my phone, which has been completely silent since last night—all the people trying to call and text out at the same time making connection almost impossible—buzzes with notification after notification. I have to stop myself from scanning to see if any of them are from Olivia. Even seeing her name right now would probably ruin me. The first one I swipe open is from the official Farmland app: The festival isn't over. A personal security guard for one of the artists accidentally left the safety off on his gun and it fired at the ground. No one was seriously hurt, though there were a number of minor injuries reported from the stampede.

I let out a slow breath. The notification says they're not canceling the final day, but security measures are going to be increased. Lines at security will likely be longer, so we need to show up earlier if we want to make it to shows on time.

There's some other information, stuff about Farmers being stronger together, about us being able to rise above it all, but I don't read it. I sit where I am, right in a patch of grass near the entrance to the Core. Farmers are walking around; some seem to be breaking down their campsites to leave later tonight and some are driving away already—both options I completely understand.

But there are plenty I can see from where I sit that are dressed and ready for the day. Not packing up, not leaving, just sitting at their campsites eating breakfast like nothing has gone wrong. The normalcy overwhelms me with a fresh rush of sadness. They look normal because scares like this *are* normal. We were lucky. Most of the time that's not the case.

When I realize I have a signal, I dial my mom without looking at any of my other notifications.

"Hey, Mom." My voice sounds shaky when I speak, so I try again. "Morning."

"Antonia, I want you to come home right now," she says in lieu of a real greeting. I can hear her moving around on the other end of the line, no doubt in the kitchen wiping down the counter-tops until she can see her reflection—the thing she always does when she's stressed. "I couldn't reach you all night and then this morning I wake up to news notifications from CNN, *Billboard*, and *Rolling Stone* saying someone was at that festival with a gun?"

Of course my mom's push notifications got to her before I did. She's probably been reading incomplete updates since last night, worried sick. I shut my eyes tight when I think about what it must have been like. Without meaning to, I've caused my mom the same kind of stress my dad did, when that's the last thing I wanted.

"Toni, are you there? Did you hear me? I want you to come home, okay, baby?"

It's the sound of her *baby* that makes me want to cry. So, I do. For the first time since the night my dad died, I cry the kind of tears that would be embarrassing if I weren't so tired and drained.

Nothing is the way it's supposed to be. Not this year, not this festival, not what's coming in the next few months. I have no idea what to do. I don't want to hurt my mom by pursuing my passion, but I'm not cut out to go to college. I didn't want to hurt Olivia in the long run, but I hurt her—and myself in the process—by breaking up with her this morning. I didn't want to allow anyone to get too close to me, but I kept reopening the same wounds from every time my dad walked out the door on his way to another tour.

It's like everything I do to reduce harm somehow makes things worse. As I sob into the phone, I'm surprised to feel the massive weight on my shoulders lift, just a little.

It feels so freeing to stop trying to contain everything, to stop trying to maintain a façade of the stoic, strong, and silent Toni Foster that I've been playing for all these years.

"Toni." My mom's voice is softer than it usually is. It's the voice she reserves for comforting me. "I'll come get you. Do you want me to drive down there? I'm driving down there, okay? Just—"

I sniffle, and laugh, just a little. Because I love my mom, and her lawyer-y need to make everything better by leaping into action. But I don't think I need that right now.

I just need an answer, one that no amount of time or live music or nights alone can seem to answer—one I've been dancing around my whole life.

"No, please. Stay. I just—Why didn't dad go to college?" I pull my knees up to my chest and rest my head on them. "Why didn't you ever tell him he had to get a different job? Some boring, normal career?"

At first it's silent on the other end, but I know she's hearing everything I'm not saying: about what college holds, about the fact that until this weekend I hadn't been able to play in months, about why I can't seem to find my footing in life. But she doesn't ask the right questions in return.

"Are you having second thoughts about IU? Is this a freshman-year panic? Because we can talk to your academic advisor about finding a major that suits you."

"No, Mom, it's not about college. It's about Dad. It's about me." I breathe out slowly. I don't want to worry her. I've never wanted her to have to worry about me. But I need her to be honest with me right now. "It's about—How was he so sure that he was supposed to be out on the road? That he wasn't supposed to be at home, with us?"

I wipe my nose with the edge of my shirt. She doesn't speak for a long while.

"It wasn't about you," she starts.

"It was about . . . restlessness." She sighs. "Your father was never satisfied. He was always chasing the next best thing. He loved you so much, Toni. But there was a hole in him that he was always trying to patch up with whatever was out there on the road." She sounds like she's thought about this a lot. Like it pains her to say it aloud. But we have to. We've gone too long without talking about this. "There's no amount of love from another person that can fill a hole like that."

I think about all those nights waiting for him to call home after a show was over and being disappointed again and again until I learned not to wait up. Until I learned not to expect anything from anyone so I couldn't ever be let down. I remember the aching feeling of longing that remained in me until I opened myself up to Olivia. I remember how being with her felt the way the best kind of song feels; like coming home.

"You are more than either of me or your dad's worst mistakes, Antonia, and heaven knows we both made plenty." I don't even breathe as I wait to hear what my mom is going to say next. "You can build a life you're proud of, and happy with, and not become your father. This isn't an either-or situation."

And I don't know if she's giving me permission, or what she'd even be giving me permission for, but I know it's what I needed to hear.

I stand up. I was wrong before. Maybe it makes sense—my trying to walk away—I don't know. What I know is that no matter where I end up next year, I want to feel forever like I felt with Olivia this weekend. Maybe love wasn't enough to make my dad feel settled, wasn't enough to make him stop running, but it can be enough for me.

"How did you know you wanted to be a lawyer?" I ask quickly.

"Other than being your mom, it's the only thing I could imagine spending my life doing. The only thing I'd want to do every day," she says without missing a beat. "Listen, are you going to be okay? I was serious when I said I'd come down to get you. You don't sound like yourself."

I nod even though she can't see me. I'm closer to being okay than I've been in nearly a year.

"Yeah, Mom," I say. I think about Olivia, about how good we could be together if I just let us. I smile. "I think I've finally figured it out."

OLIVIA

SUNDAY AFTERNOON

The sun has risen higher in the sky and the people around us are bustling, headed home or to enjoy what's left of Farmland. But I'm not paying attention to any of that; I'm focused on the way my skin prickles with the thrill of being the sole object of someone's attention. Being someone that can hold attention, that can be wanted, even for a second, manages to stop the restlessness that I feel.

I turn to Peter with a coy smile plastered on. It doesn't even feel right on my face anymore. I'm putting on a costume. I hate it. I need it.

"Okay but what about *Infinity on High*? You can't seriously tell me that *Infinity on High* isn't in your top three of their best albums ever!" he says.

"You're cute when you get all worked up." My voice doesn't even sound like mine. I'm someone else.

Peter's eyebrows wrinkle together. "Huh?"

"I said"—I move my hand to his chin, tilt his face to mine—"you're cute when you're all worked up."

Peter swallows slowly and his pupils dilate. He starts to lean forward, and I know I've done it. I've got him to want to kiss me. But the excitement that usually comes in this moment doesn't. The endorphins stay dormant. If I just push a little further, maybe I can capture it again.

I angle my face toward his, and I move in slowly, seductively. I tilt his chin just right so that I can almost—

"Wait, hold on—" Peter's head snaps back before we make contact, like he's coming out of a trance, but it's not quick enough.

"Olivia?" comes a voice to my right. My stomach drops.

"Oh my God," comes a voice to Peter's left. He looks over his shoulder and immediately stands up. I clench my teeth.

I don't have to look to know who the voices belong to. Actually, there's nothing I want to do less than look right now. But Peter runs in her direction and I know this is happening.

"Toni, this isn't— Just wait a second!" he calls.

I push myself to standing and see Toni's back as she rushes away, with Imani running in the opposite direction. The buzzing in my ears intensifies until it drowns out every other noise in my head. My mom through tears, *Why can't you be more like your sister, Olivia?* Troy's voice whispering in my ear at that first party, *If you cared about me, you would.* The constant monologue I have running saying: *You're not enough. You'll never be enough.*

But one thought holds tight through all the rest of it: *Everything I touch, I break.*

Choosing whether to go after Imani or Toni isn't a choice at all. Toni has already decided that I'm not worth wanting, but Imani is my best friend. Imani has to take me back.

"Imani, please! Wait up!" I race to catch up to her. She's already managed to walk nearly halfway to the Core in the time since she stormed away.

I know I shouldn't have made a move on Peter, not when I told her I wouldn't so much as bat my eyes at anyone this weekend. I promised her a best friend weekend, and I didn't deliver. She should be a little mad at me for that. I deserve it.

But it's not like *she* wanted to date Peter—she told him as much. So, she can't be that mad that I kissed him. Or almost-kissed him. Whatever.

At least with Imani there's room to apologize, to figure things out. It's not like the two of us have never gotten into it, after all. But with me and Toni, it's clear that ship has sailed. There's no hope left there. It was bleak before the thing with Peter, but some things are too extreme to ever come back from.

And kissing someone's best friend, even if it only almost happened, is the type of thing that means no return.

And maybe that's why I did it. Like how the devil you know is better than the devil you don't, maybe the loneliness you choose is better than the loneliness that's chosen for you.

"Peter said you turned him down." I stop in front of her and hold my hands out to keep her from going any farther. The quick jog has already left me a little breathless, so I take a puff of my inhaler quickly before continuing between breaths. "I would never try and, like, take your man from you. I know that doesn't make this much better but—"

"You think this is about a guy I barely know?" Imani's voice is hard, pressed steel, a voice she saves for cursing out my exes in the hallways or for getting restaurant managers to take her seriously when she wants a refund on her undercooked chicken piccata. Never for me. "Of course you do. Because that's where your mind always is, on finding a new object of infatuation. You don't care about gender, whether the two of you have anything in common, your own well-being—nothing matters to you, does it?"

"Whoa. Um." It's like a gut punch, hearing her say it so plainly.

I've known that Imani doesn't agree with a lot of my decisions—has actively warned me off most of them—but I didn't think she thought so little of me. Like I'm some inflated caricature of a confused bisexual, just running from person to person because I can't make up my mind. It's something my mom would say, or Nia, but never my best friend.

"That's kind of harsh, Mani." I flex my fingers and try to think past the rushing in my head.

I made Imani a promise when we came to Farmland that I wouldn't do what I've done before—abandon her and leave her to fend for herself. And I didn't. While I was with Toni, she was having fun with Peter! She was happy . . . I thought.

I think back to the first night where he crashed in my sleeping bag. It seemed like they were vibing. They like the same music and are able to switch between commentary on the history of Pop Top just as easily as they can the science of photoluminescence or Calvin Coolidge's pet raccoon. How was I supposed to know that she not only wasn't interested in him, but felt like I'd pawned her off on him so I could run off into the sunset with Toni?

She leans back like I've slapped her. "Harsh?"

"Yes, *harsh*." I cross my arms over my chest and widen my stance. Maybe if I look solid, my inside will reflect my outside. "And you're being kind of biphobic. Just because my sexuality is more fluid than other people's doesn't mean—"

"You don't get to lecture me about being a good person right now," she seethes.

"Look, can we just make up, please? This has honestly been a really hard day for me, and I kind of just want to cry and eat a taco from that cart in the Core."

Imani's face shifts so quickly and so drastically into outrage, I take a step back on instinct. My stomach clenches.

"How is this somehow about you too?"

"What do you . . . what do you mean?" I can feel tears welling up at my eyelids, threatening to spill over.

"I mean exactly what I said, Olivia. Every person in your life is just another funhouse mirror to show you different, more entertaining versions of yourself for a little while." She throws her hands out to her sides. "It's always about you. *Your* feelings. *Your* heartache. How can you use this person to feel good about yourself for fifteen minutes until you get bored, get dumped, and then move on? Lather, rinse and repeat."

I want to argue, to say it's not like that, that I've never thought of her as a means to an end. But maybe she's right. Maybe there's some truth in what she's saying. Maybe I am the problem, just not in the way I've been thinking. My mind immediately jumps to Troy, and it feels like I'm breathing through a straw.

"Troy is a different story," she says—always too in tune with my emotions, even now. "You didn't deserve that. No one does."

It's silent for a second. Or, at least as silent as it can be at a music festival.

"It's just—You're not a character in a movie, okay? You're a real girl. You don't get a montage where you buy a new wardrobe and suddenly everything changes. This is your life. You are who you are." She pushes her sunglasses up on top of her hair and presses her hands to her eyes. She doesn't look at me as she adds, "Your problem isn't that you're too much or too extra, or whatever it is you think scares people away. The people you date are just assholes. Your problem is that you're selfish."

"Imani, I'm—"

She cuts her eyes at me, and they're more than a little watery.

"Sorry? You should've said that that time I had floor seats to see my favorite band, and instead of watching them perform, I left to talk you down from yet another crisis because *you really thought Aaron was the one and now you're going to be alone forever.*"

"But you said—"

She rolls her eyes. "You really believed that me, of all people, would make the mistake of buying phony tickets? I said that because it made me sound less pathetic than the truth."

Her fists clench at her sides and I wish for a second she would just punch me or something. Let's just get it out of the way, just have it out, because anything would be better than this. This hurts more than any uppercut could, and she's clearly not done yet. Now that she says it, I can see it so clearly. I've done this so many times over the course of our friendship, she could probably go on forever.

"Or how about the time you made me come to Chicago with you to help you recover from a breakup, and you abandoned me in a dirty basement—after listening to a terrible band play—surrounded by skeevy dudes trying to touch me for *four hours* without telling me where you were? Meanwhile you were off making out with their lead guitarist?" Her whole body is rigid. "I was so scared, Olivia. And you didn't even bother to keep track of the rings we got on that trip—the only good part of the whole weekend."

She twists the silver pinky ring around until it slips off. I didn't think she noticed that mine had gone missing. But there's a lot I underestimated about Imani. She closes her fingers around it as she says, "Or what about the time you picked looking for a stupid *apple*— a contest which is probably canceled by the way—over riding the Ferris wheel with me? The only thing I wanted to do in this hellhole. So, no. It's too late for your sorry. I don't fucking forgive you for this."

She starts walking, toward nothing in particular but away from me, which must be enough for her. She stops suddenly, spins, and takes two steps back in my direction, pointing.

"No, you know what? I can't even blame you. This isn't even on you. This is on me."

"Imani, no. It's my fault, I—"

She keeps going, almost as if she's not even speaking to me anymore.

"I just kept holding your hand through every heartbreak, just kept thinking, *At some point she'll get it. She'll understand what she means to me. Next time, she'll choose me.*" She laughs. "But you were never going to get it, were you?"

I—What? My mouth goes dry.

"I think I've been in love with you since the day we met."

Her voice breaks and it's too much for me to handle. Imani doesn't cry, not ever. And it's so horrible, all of this, the whole terrible, awful, mess of it. Because I loved her too, that first day in Honors Geometry, when she raised her hand and answered that first question with such sureness I knew she was the type of person that I'd be stupid not to hold on to. She was so smart, so solid, and she's been that every day since.

I just don't love her the way that she loves me. *Loved* me, past tense now, surely.

We're standing in the middle of the gravel road, and a blue sedan crunches the ground behind us, trying to get out. We step to the side so we're standing in the grass, and Imani doesn't rip into me again. She doesn't say anything for a while. And I don't know what to say. So the two of us just stare at each other until her deceptively calm voice pipes up.

"I came to tell you that I've decided to stay to see Kittredge." I reach forward to take hold of her, somehow. Like maybe she won't leave me if I can just cling to her for a second longer. She jerks her arm back as I get closer. "Don't"—she starts with a snap—"Don't touch me, okay?"

She closes her eyes and angles her face up to the sky. It's graying quickly, the weather somehow managing to capture the way this moment feels in the most cliché of all movie clichés. Another breakup scene in my life, flanked by disaster. God, I'm a walking made-for-TV tragedy, huh?

"The minute Kittredge is done performing, I'm leaving." Imani wipes at her cheeks. "I'm not going to miss my favorite band again because of you."

She doesn't wait for me to respond. She just turns away, opens her fist, and lets her ring fall to the dirt with an inaudible thud.

And it's that, the cheap little ring that meant enough to her to wear it every day for over a year, discarded like trash, that breaks me.

As she walks in the direction of nothing in particular, leaving me standing there surrounded by all the things I couldn't say, I hiccup through my sobs. All my apologies and explanations so jumbled and messy that I don't know how to put any of it into words.

I don't walk back to camp or head to the Core after her. I sit right there in the grass where I was standing, and watch Farmers heading back to their campsites and then some of the people who've already packed up camp and are getting ready to leave. I pick the ring up and try to shine it on the hem of my dress before slipping it on my own finger.

Imani knows me better than anyone, and I'm supposed to know her just as well. So how did I manage to miss every glaring, screaming sign in front of me for the past three years that said she had feelings for me? While I was consumed with finding The Right Person—or just The Person, depending on the day—I was driving a knife even further into my best friend's heart. I made everything about me, sucked all the air out of every room we shared together.

She was right to be angry with me. Furious, in fact. I know I got off easy, even, after everything I'd done over the past few years. Imani had been the best friend I could've asked for, showed up for me every time I needed her. But I never returned that to her the way I should have.

I was wrong. When Toni said all those things about what I deserve and what I should accept for myself, it was because she wasn't seeing the version of me that the people who know me the best see. The version Imani sees—the version my mom or Nia see. She couldn't have been.

I'm supposed to be a master of love; it's supposed to be the one thing I know better than anything else. But if love really means showing up, I couldn't even do that.

I look at the notificationless screen on my phone—no one's thinking about me enough to hit me up, not even the trolls on Confidential.

I'm really and truly alone.

Exactly as I deserve to be.

TONI

SUNDAY AFTERNOON

When I see Peter and Olivia pressed close together, practically kissing, all I can feel is the wreckage.

Me and Olivia are over. My only friend betrayed me. Farmland is gone.

I run away from camp faster than I think I've ever run before. I dodge Peter's shouting and following after me by hiding behind an RV, and then keep going without the worry of him at my heels. There's nothing he could say to me right now that I'd want to hear. Nothing he could say to me that would make this feeling go away.

It begins as a hollowness, some rattling emptiness that tells me maybe there was nothing there all along. Maybe I wasn't pretending to be the ice queen, maybe the pretending only happened when I thought I could be the type of person capable of loving someone. Capable of letting someone in. But I walk. And I walk. And with every step, that emptiness evolves, changes and changes, fills and fills until I'm brimming with something else, something I'm afraid I can't contain.

I'm angry. I'm suddenly so overwhelmingly, wildly angry that my vision blurs. My palms sweat. I stop where I'm standing—no regard for the Farmers who are walking behind me on the path to the Core—and try to collect myself. But I can't.

How dare this girl smile at me, and stick around even after I tried to shake her, and talk and talk and talk and talk until she'd leapt over all my defenses? How dare she be funny and open and laugh like I was more than a cardboard cutout of a person, like she really cared about me? How dare she be everything I didn't know I wanted, change the way I thought about myself, make me want to be more honest more open more bold more more more?

How dare I fall in love with her, knowing what I know about what love makes of us?

How dare I be so stupid?

I walk toward the security gates that lead into the Core, and as I go, the moments leading up to now flash through my head like Olivia's Polaroids. Snapshots of memories, frozen in time. Olivia dancing in the grass during Odd One's set. Peter with his tongue out near the Goldspur performance barn. Imani and Olivia with their arms around each other in line for the hydration station yesterday. Everything in those memories now has a stillness. An ignorance.

By the time I reach the line for security outside the Core, the festival is coming to life again. Folks are walking to and from the showers, people strumming their guitars aimlessly outside their tents. People don't wave as easily as they used to. They don't smile at each other as broadly. Everyone in line for security is jittery and quiet. A young guy in a Hawaiian shirt reaches for his shorts pocket to grab his phone and the woman beside him gasps, and then looks embarrassed by her reaction.

It takes about thirty minutes for me to get through security, but I don't mind. The monotony of the process is a welcome distraction.

I don't know what I'm heading to until I'm there, standing in front of it. The Granny Smith stage looms large in front of me, quiet and peaceful. Later tonight, Kittredge will perform here in front of tens of thousands of screaming fans and Farmers. Twenty years ago, my dad performed here with the Red Hot Chili Peppers after winning the Golden Apple.

I use the hem of my shirt to wipe my eyes. I'm not crying in earnest, just a few stray tears, but it's already too much.

I wonder who won the Golden Apple, or whether or not they're even going to do it anymore. Maybe that too has been snuffed out with the events of the past day. I don't want to think about leaving, or being stuck in a car with Peter, the last person I thought I'd ever feel this betrayed by, for eight hours, but I can't stand to stay here much longer. Once we leave this place, I'm leaving behind whatever memories it holds. I don't want them anymore.

My phone buzzes in my pocket, and I can't help myself from hoping it's Olivia. And once I do, I hate myself for even having the thought. It's an unknown number, but I answer it out of curiosity.

"Yeah?"

"Toni Jackson. How ya doing?" Davey Mack's scratchy tenor rings through the line. My heart upticks at the sound.

I've never spoken to him before—never had reason to—but I know his voice well from interviews, from Kittredge's songs on the radio. It's been years since I even saw him in person. Probably since the band played Lollapalooza three years ago, and my mom took me up to Chicago to see my dad and I watched their show from the pit.

"Davey Mack," I breathe out. I try to sound as cool as possible. Even though he's not-so-distantly been a part of my universe thanks to my dad for years, we don't know each other. And he's still one of the biggest stars in the world. "What's—What's up?"

"Well, I wanted to personally say that you did a great job at the Golden Apple yesterday," he says. "You and Olivia were something special. A power duo! Is she there? I have good news for you both."

I cringe. "No, um, no. Yeah no, she's not."

"Oh damn! I wanted to get the two of you in the same place. Well, you'll tell her, right? I'd like to have you perform with us tonight if you're down."

I'm pretty sure I stop speaking, or breathing even. He offers a few more pleasantries, kind words about my talent and where to show up later, but the call is over quickly. He speaks to me friendly, but there's no indication that he knows who I am or, better yet, whose daughter I am. This is it. I did it. I won the Golden Apple. It feels even better to me knowing that I managed this with no link to my dad's relationship to the band.

After hanging up, even though I'll deny it if anyone ever asks, I scream. I scream, and it's high-pitched and embarrassing. I can't even begin to wrap my head around what this means. I get to perform, on stage, during Kittredge's headline set tonight. I get to have my name on that ridiculously long plaque near the entrance, the same one my dad's name was burned into twenty years prior. This is unbelievable. *I have to call Ol—*

My heart sinks. I want to call Olivia, to celebrate with her—thank her for getting me here. But of course I can't. I don't have it in me to revel in this victory with her, and I definitely can't play alongside her tonight. We're not even speaking. And now that she and Peter are whatever she and Peter are, I don't know if she'd want to, even if I could bring myself to consider it.

What good is the music if you don't get to share it with the person who makes you want to sing in the first place?

OLIVIA

SUNDAY AFTERNOON

I walk back and flop down on the ground in what used to be our campsite.

The only thing that Imani hasn't already packed into the car is my bag. It's so targeted, her message so clear, that I can't help myself; I start crying again.

I thought my pain and the way I loved and ached to be loved in return was unique, was something that deserved to take up space not only in my life, but in her life as well. And that's not what it means to love someone. I ruined things with my best friend and shattered any chance of ever being on good terms with Toni again—I destroyed two relationships in one fell swoop. A new personal best.

There's an ache in my chest that's unlike anything I've felt after a breakup before. This is different, bone-deep, the kind of hurt that can't be fixed with ice cream and a movie marathon. Those were Band-Aids for how to heal my surface-level hurt. But for something this intrinsic, I don't know what to do. I don't know how you bounce back from something like this.

I unzip my fanny pack and grab my inhaler to take a quick puff, because crying always upsets my asthma. My hand brushes across the pointed edges of my Polaroids as I reach inside. I pull them out and spread them across the grass in front of me.

As I shuffle through the photos, it occurs to me that the fifth apple is still out there somewhere. For something I spent my entire weekend racing toward, winning the car has managed to become so insignificant in the face of everything else that it's almost nonexistent. I mean, winning would still be nice, but the urgency is gone.

Still, I check the page and the hashtag to see if anyone has found the last apple out of curiosity. It's been a while since I looked at the @FoundAtFarmland page, and when I pull it up now, after the final clue, there are a number of black boxes with simple text: Fear Has No Place at Farmland.

The lightheartedness that the page used to contain—pictures of smiling Farmers at the Fiat booth in the Core nestled between clues—is gone. It seems as though while I was busy unraveling what good was left in my own life, someone was busy doing the same to this space of joy and community.

When I leave Instagram, I decide to do a full sweep of all my socials. I don't know what possesses me to check Confidential. The rational part of my brain tells me to avoid it like the plague. But right now, I can't help myself. It's almost compulsive, an old habit that I thought I'd kicked, logging in and scanning my account.

I expect the usual trolls to be camped out in my notifications like usual, but instead, there's only one: direct messages from @KMitch03. I nervously twist Imani's ring around my pinky, like her anxious habit has somehow transferred to me.

It made sense when I saw that Troy had moved on to Kayla barely two weeks after our breakup. From her homecoming queen title to the state tennis championship she'd just led Park Meade to, Kayla's face could've been plastered on the cover of the Good Girl Bible. She made good choices, always did the right thing. She would never do anything as stupid as what I did. And if she did, Troy would never betray her like that.

That kind of thing doesn't happen to Good Girls. I close my eyes for a second before I open the message, trying to get my bearings. Whatever she has to say to me, about me, I can handle it. I won't use it as fuel to spark my next bad decision. This time, I won't burn my life down just to rise from the ashes as something different like Imani said. It's not worth it. Not when it costs me the people I can't imagine my life without.

From @KMitch03 to @OliviaTwist:

Hey so ik we're not friends or whatever but you're the only person I think would get it so I didn't know what else to do

My breath quickens at the first message, this time for an entirely different reason than before. Besides Troy, Kayla and I don't have anything else in common and never had.

What you said he did? I know he did it

I clutch my phone so tight I'm afraid the plastic of my case might crack in my hands. I can feel the early prickling of sweat dotting the back of my hairline.

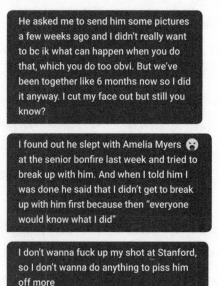

He asked me to send him some pictures a few weeks ago and I didn't really want to bc ik what can happen when you do that, which you do too obvi. But we've been together like 6 months now so I did it anyway. I cut my face out but still you know?

I found out he slept with Amelia Myers 😱 at the senior bonfire last week and tried to break up with him. And when I told him I was done he said that I didn't get to break up with him first because then "everyone would know what I did"

I don't wanna fuck up my shot at Stanford, so I don't wanna do anything to piss him off more

There's no way. I don't have a reason to believe that Kayla would make any of this up—I mean what reason would she have to paint herself into the same corner I'm in unless it was the truth?

But still, I struggle to wrap my head around it. How could something like this happen to someone like her? Someone flawless and smart and perfectly matched for Troy and his set?

From the moment the news came out, my mom had made it abundantly clear that she would rather sweep what happened under the rug than risk her job. Nia made no secret about the fact that if I wouldn't have done something so irresponsible in the first place, I wouldn't have embarrassed our family like I had.

So I compromised, something between dropping it completely and taking legal action. I thought it would keep things quieter, maybe make everything less messy. I put it in the hands of the school. I let them set a date for a judicial hearing, and then watched as they set another one when that date no longer worked, again and again for months. Until one day, it was the end of my junior year, Troy was already being tapped by Duke and UNC and Ohio State, and my mother had barely spoken to me since the day Troy posted the pictures. There was no resolution and would never be. Because no one cared about girls like me.

Even when they didn't say it explicitly, I knew the truth: there's nothing you can do with Black girls who aren't "respectable" and easy to understand and the best at everything. We're disposable.

All this time, I've been told I deserved what happened to me. That I was too much, too *me* to deserve the same type of love and respect as girls like Kayla. But since what she's saying is true, then it wasn't me at all.

Toni's words from last night come rushing back to me with so much force it catches me off guard: *That big love you give everyone else—you deserve to save some for yourself. You're worth that much.*

You're worth that much.

Kayla is worth that much. I'm worth that much. Every woman is worth that much.

And until boys like Troy that grow into men with too much power and too much ego are made to face what they've done, this will keep happening. I don't know what I'm going to say at the judicial hearing on Friday, but I know this: I'm worth more than Troy winning Park Meade another state championship.

My thumbs are hovering over the reply box when two more messages pop up back to back.

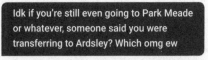

I leave Confidential and open up the camera app instead. Maybe I can't fix what happened between me and Imani, maybe me and Toni were never meant to be, but I can keep this from happening to another girl. I can make sure everyone knows exactly what type of creep Troy is—how he's preyed on girls and used our bodies as bargaining chips in his game for power. Waiting for the school to do the right thing hasn't worked, and me ignoring it hasn't helped anything either. I can't leave my life, my happiness, in the hands of other people. This is one thing I'm going to have to do on my own.

If people want to spread a story, *my* story, then they can spread the one I tell. The version I control.

I roll my shoulders back, fix my mascara, and press record.

"At the beginning of my junior year, I started dating Troy Murphy, the starting forward for the Park Meade High School varsity boys' basketball team," I start, attempting to make my voice sound more assured than I feel. "That fall, he violated my privacy in the worst way possible."

I tell the entire story. I maintain eye contact with the camera and imagine that I'm looking right at him. I want him to see me and understand the depths of what he did. I want him to be afraid. I refuse to be ashamed.

Once I upload this, there will be no more secrets. My mom will know I haven't been at a church retreat all weekend. Everyone at Park Meade will know what Troy did to me, and it'll be up to them to decide whether or not to ignore it. Whether or not to decide to keep supporting someone like him. That will be their burden to bear, not mine. I can't let my mom's job, or my classmates' outrage, or my sister's pride keep me from the life I deserve. Even if the people who should have didn't stand up for me when I needed them most, I can stand up for me right now.

I open Confidential.

And before I can second-guess myself, I press send.

TONI

SUNDAY AFTERNOON

My phone starts buzzing in my back pocket, and I consider just letting it go. When I check the screen I swipe unlock.

"Hey." My voice comes out raspy, a little hoarse from the celebratory screaming.

"Toni, oh my God, I'm so glad you answered!" It's Mack's voice, loud and concerned. "You're good, right? How's Olivia? Where are you both? I wanted to check in after everything that happened yesterday, but no one had a signal last night and it was a whole thing. You can come to the bus and hang out with us until the show if you want. It's kinda lonely around here right now because the whole team is out—"

"Everything is fine," I say, interrupting.

My gut roils at the lie, but I want to stop the runaway train that is her concern. We haven't seen or spoken to each other in years, so her alarm shocks me. Why does she care what happened to a girl she knew briefly when she was a kid?

I don't understand it, but I consider the offer. I think it might be a good idea to be around someone else instead of retreating further into myself.

"Where are you?"

She runs off instructions on how to get to where their tour bus is located and says she'll meet me at the gate so I can get through without the proper wristband, and we hang up.

It doesn't take more than ten minutes before I reach the back lot where the tour buses are kept.

"Toni!" Mack runs past the security guards manning the entrance and pulls me in for a hug. I guess everything is different in the wake of the world feeling like it's falling to pieces.

"It's so good you're here. I'm sure you heard that the band is going on tonight. It's been super chaotic, but chaotic good, you know, not chaotic evil," she rushes out as we walk through another set of security guards. More modest this time because they lead into a more exclusive area, but still. "The band is making all these plans for their set tonight. It's going to be great."

One of the security guards insists on patting me down, and I agree to it while gritting my teeth. I understand the need, but the touching unnerves me. The physical closeness feels unnatural, even though it's entirely professional and perfunctory. A few days ago, I couldn't even bring myself to hug people with my whole self thrown into it. Until . . .

I try not to think about Olivia, but every thought circles back to her. I can't help myself. In less than seventy-two hours she has become this magnificent cacophony, and without her around, the silence feels suffocating. Just as I thought allowing myself to open up to somebody besides Peter or my mom would hurt, it does. Even more than I imagined.

We reach the doors to the bus and Mack puts a hand on my shoulder and it's only then that I realize I'm crying. I'm now the kind of person who cries in front of other people without even noticing. Great.

"You okay?"

I look to the side and close my eyes to the incoming tears.

I can feel Mack's thin arms wrapping around me from the back, and she holds me for as long as I need to be held. And when I'm done, I get it. What my dad's Truths mean. Why we return to music for the answers when we can't find them ourselves. In that moment, there's only one thing I can do.

"Can I borrow a guitar for a second?" I wipe my eyes. Mack immediately maneuvers around me to grab the acoustic just sitting on the table.

"I have a song I need to write."

* / * *

Finishing a song for the first time in eight months feels like someone has removed a brick that's been resting on my chest. I knew my breaths had been coming in shorter, but until it was gone, I couldn't remember what it was like to exhale without it.

It takes about an hour, all together, to try to find language to capture the way I feel. The notes come easily though. That part has always been the most natural for me—finding the right chords to match what I'm trying to say. It reminds me of Olivia matching those almost-lyrics to her photos. But now the thought doesn't feel like a weight, it feels a bit like a light. Like I can see more clearly what I couldn't before this afternoon, before this weekend, at all.

The bus is currently empty, and I feel like an interloper, an intruder, sitting here with I-don't-know-who's guitar in my hands, but Mack keeps assuring me it's okay.

Most of the guys from the band are apparently out and about on the grounds, joining in the volunteer effort to clean up what was damaged in the chaos after the misfire, while Teela and Davey are at the Farmland on-site office having conference calls with their manager, agent, and the festival organizers to work out how best to move forward. Mack has been on FaceTime with her girlfriend for most of the time, holed up in one of the bunks in the back, trying to get her to believe that she's safe.

She plops down next to me while I plunk out some notes, trying to figure out if I've got the bridge right or if there's just something slightly off about it. "You should try an A minor there instead of the F," she says. I try it, and she's right. The difference is minute, but just enough. It finally sounds right.

"Teela wants to get the other headliners to join them tonight. Sonny Blue, Pop Top, Odd Ones—everybody who's still here—to play a massive, all-night set."

It sounds like the type of thing my dad would've stood behind. If live music was the altar that he laid himself prostrate before, then he'd be damned before letting fear of what could have been desecrate his house of worship. The way Teela and Davey are working on reclaiming the festival feels more like a memorial than his own funeral had.

"You think people are going to stay through the end of the night?" I ask.

"Yeah, I really do." Mack nods too hard and one of the drumsticks that she has lodged through her topknot slips out and clatters on the floor. She picks it up and starts spinning it through her fingers so quickly it's clearly second-nature to her. "I overheard—"

Someone bangs at the door so loudly, both of us jump to our feet. Mack holds the drumstick in her hand like a baseball bat and approaches the door slowly. She looks through the window before deciding to open it. I set the guitar down and stand, just in case whoever's coming in is the type of person I might need to fend off with my aggressive stare or surprisingly strong left hook.

But the person who trails Mack inside isn't someone I want to punch at all.

I may have, two hours ago, but now seeing Peter just makes me sad.

"Toni, Jesus, I've been looking everywhere for you. You wouldn't answer your phone!"

"How did you even get back here, Peter?" I cross my arms and lean against the table as casually as possible.

"You'd think the security would be a little more careful with checking the inside of the trash bins they haul in and out of VIP." He shakes his hair a little so it's out of his face, and a piece of lettuce falls out. He puts his hat back on. "I had to find you, dude. You have to know I would never—"

"How exactly did you find me?" I interrupt.

He holds up his cell. "I have your Find My iPhone information, remember?" He at least has the decency to look a little embarrassed as he adds, "I wouldn't have done it unless this were an emergency, okay? Also I have *got* to know how you ended up on Kittredge's tour bus, but whatever, that's a story for another time."

I look over his shoulder to where Mack is standing. It was cool of her to invite me to camp out here and let me cry without asking any questions, but this is a conversation I should probably have in private. She squeezes my shoulder in support and backs herself into the bunk area while pushing in her AirPods.

"I don't care, okay?" I say, sitting down on the edge of the couch. "Just . . . I don't want to hear it."

"No but T, please. I need you to hear it. You're my best friend. You know that. I—" He stops. He pulls his hat off and twists it around in his hands. "Everything was all over the place. I was still angry, and scared, and then Imani texted and I was just . . . I shouldn't have even gotten that close to kissing Olivia. I know that." He sits down next to me and his face is more serious than I've ever seen it. "I'll never stop feeling like the lowest of the low garbage for even letting it go as far as it did. I'm sorry, T."

I don't want to forgive him. I still feel the sting of betrayal, and I don't know if I'm ready to let it go.

"I've never lied to you, right? Like, you know me better than that. I'm not lying now. Okay?"

I allow my eyes a second to really examine him, this guy that I thought was my best friend. Peter has always been painfully earnest, almost to the point of causing me secondhand embarrassment. He cries openly at romantic movies when we have FaceTime Netflix nights. He stops to pet every dog he meets on the street. He didn't think twice when I asked him to come to this festival with me because I just knew it would change my life.

Peter Menon, I realize, is the most consistent thing in my life.

I think about my new song, about the Truths I've collected this weekend between sets and stolen moments behind barns. I think about what I want from my life, and the people I want in it. And I say, "Okay." I swallow the lump in my throat and say it again, more firmly. "Okay, Menon. Pull shit like that again—or *almost* pull shit like that again—and I will go full '04 Van Halen and take my guitar to your face. Deal?"

"Yes! Oh my God, thank you! I've never been happier to have

someone threaten my bodily autonomy." Peter falls forward and bows dramatically instead of hugging me like I know he wants to. Still giving me space when I need it, even without me asking for it. "I was so worried I was going to have to send back those matching denim jackets I got airbrushed with our faces on them for your eighteenth birthday. They cost me, like, a semester's worth of minimum wage at the Java Hut."

I laugh, because I can't help myself. But it only takes a second before I remember why I sunk so low before. So even if Peter didn't kiss Olivia, it sure as hell looked like she wanted to kiss him, and that's a whole separate issue.

"Can I say something?" He moves to sit next to me on the couch.

"When has permission ever stopped you before?"

"Good point." He looks at me seriously for a second. Outside the bus, I can hear the gentle *plink plink plink* of rain hitting the siding. "You know why I like memorizing facts about dead presidents?"

"Because you're odd." I shrug. I've never really wondered why Peter does the things he does. I learned to accept all his spots just like he learned to accept all my cracks, without question.

"Okay, yes, sure, that's not entirely wrong." He rolls his eyes and grins. "But more than that, it's a way to make sense of things. This country was founded by weirdos and jerks and the dullest knives in the drawer." I think back to some of the facts he's shared about all those white men over the course of our friendship, and he's right on every count. "And yet, they managed to convince the world that this country is some kind of global superpower."

"I think racism is also to blame for that," I add.

"Oh, for sure." He laughs. "I guess what I'm saying is, I like knowing that these guys were train wrecks. If they could be trusted with this whole"—he circles a finger in the air—"*thing*, why shouldn't we trust ourselves with all the other stuff?"

I close my eyes and shake my head. I should have known he'd find a way to therapize me before the weekend was over. His face is serious when I look at him again.

"You saying I should trust myself with someone's heart, Menon?"

"No, I'm saying you should trust her with yours." He bumps his shoulder against mine. "You really like Olivia, right? I mean, whatever happened earlier aside and everything. You want to keep her around?"

There's no use lying to Peter. He knows the answer anyway— I'm sure it's written in the very line of my body, the way I can feel myself go more alert at the sound of her name.

"So what? You're a mess sometimes. We all are. Does that mean it's not still worth a shot?"

Peter is a perpetual optimist, so I usually take his advice with a grain of salt. But on this point, I have to concede. The fact is, no matter how hard I try to convince myself otherwise, I can't bring myself to stay angry at her.

I'm mostly angry at myself for even thinking that breaking up this morning would be enough to turn off the part of my brain that had fallen for her. I'm angry because I waited so many years to allow myself to feel the way that I felt around her because I thought that loneliness was somehow the antidote to heartbreak.

But I know better now than I did before: loneliness only begets more loneliness—it doesn't protect you from hurting. Maybe that's where love comes in. The risk of the hurt is offset by the rest of it. By the nights you spend dancing in barns, by the afternoons you spend shouting along to your favorite band's lyrics in an audience of ten thousand other people just as passionate about them as you are, or by the mornings you wake up nestled against each other in a too-warm tent.

When my dad said I was going to be big one day, maybe he was talking about music. But maybe he wasn't. Maybe he meant that I was destined to love big, to care about another person and have that care be mutual. The idea of that still frightens me to my core.

"What if one person can only lose so much before they fall apart completely?" I ask.

"I don't know, man," he says. "But I've gotta believe the people I have left will love me enough to try and put me back together again."

I nod. I think this is what it means for music to give us answers. Olivia is some kind of melody that has made a song of my universe, and I realize I want to spend whatever time I may have trying to figure out all the notes. I don't want to rearrange them, but I can't think of many things better than appreciating their beauty.

"So." He nods to the guitar on the table and the hastily scrawled lyrics next to me. "You gonna pick those pieces up now or what?"

"Peter," I say. "I'm going to need your help making a plan."

I'm going to call in every favor I have. I'm going to make good on the first lesson my dad ever taught me: that anything could be solved with live music. I'm going to do what I'm most afraid of.

I'm going to get Olivia back.

OLIVIA

SUNDAY EVENING

"What are you doing here?" Imani stands up from the cooler she's sitting on when I arrive. I freeze where I'm standing. She doesn't look as enraged as she was before, but she certainly doesn't look happy to see me. I immediately feel cowed, even though I didn't even come here for her. I came here because I was asked.

"Peter said he needed me to meet him here."

I look down at the text from Peter that asked me and Imani to be back at camp in a half hour. It sounded urgent, without its usual emojis and memes, so I fired back a response.

"I'm sorry." I sent an audio iMessage so he could understand I thought this was worth a longer conversation. "I was completely out of line earlier. That wasn't fair to you. Or to Imani, although for way different reasons, and . . . I just, I'm sorry. It won't happen again."

"I know it won't, friendo. I was off my game too," he sent back quickly. "It'd be pretty awkward if we kissed, since you and my sister from another mister are gonna get back together, you know?"

I didn't tell him that there was no way that was going to happen, that me and Toni were well and officially done before I tried to kiss him.

Standing before Imani now though, I wish Peter would've just told me whatever he needed to tell me earlier. Either that, or I wish I'd had the foresight not to show up five minutes early. Imani is *always* fifteen minutes early. It's the Capricorn in her.

"Same. I wish he'd just texted whatever he wanted to say instead of all these cloak-and-dagger theatrics. Kittredge goes on in a bit and I want to get a good spot." She looks at her phone to double-check the time. She adds under her breath, "And then I can finally leave this germ-infested wasteland."

She sits back down on the cooler. Well, more like plops down, like her body is too heavy for her to hold up anymore. She doesn't even look angry now, she just looks . . . depleted. The sight breaks my heart. And even though I know it's not nearly enough, I have to tell her the truth.

"I'm sorry," I blurt out.

Welp. There goes my heartfelt speech.

She rubs her temples. "Seriously, Olivia. We don't have to do this. I get it."

"How could you when I didn't even get it until, like, an hour ago?" I rush forward and sit on the small space next to her. I think belatedly that it might be too close for comfort, given the circumstances, but Imani doesn't shove me onto my ass right away, so I take that as a good sign. "I have been a nightmare person since the day we met."

She looks over at me and drops her hands into her lap. I keep going.

"You're the best person I know. And I know that's maybe a massive thing to say to someone, but I mean it. You are the first person I think about calling when I have news. The last text I send every night before I go to bed." It's not a struggle to come up with things I love about Imani, or reasons why I want to salvage this friendship.

"You're a literal, certifiable genius. It's proven. You have the second-highest GPA in Park Meade history, I checked—second to only my big sister, by the way, which I can work out in therapy when I get back home—but you don't make other people feel small or stupid with how big your brain is. It's just, you know, another thing that makes you *you*." I search Imani's face for some sort of understanding. "But . . ."

"But you don't love me like I love you," she finishes.

I shake my head sadly. At the end of the day, that's just the heart of it. I can't show up for Imani like that, because I just don't feel it.

But I can show up for her as the best friend who ever friended, which I plan on doing until we're both old and gray and marching in Pride parades side by side as those iconic old ladies with the best signs and fabulously tacky rainbow outfits. We have a lot we need to figure out about how to navigate this new dynamic between us, the both of us moving forward completely honestly for the first time ever, but I think we can do it.

She shakes her head and looks up at the sky before sighing one of those signature Imani sighs.

"I've been thinking about how you leave your dirty socks in my room sometimes when you sleep over, and how you think pineapple on pizza is an acceptable topping."

"It's criminally underrated, Imani, and you *know* that," I say.

"No, it's literally just criminal, but that's not the point." She smooths down her hair and sweeps it all over one shoulder. "The point is: I think I may have been unfair to you too. I elevated you to this, you know, pedestal—looked at you like a *thing* that I deserved to obtain one day. Like I earned it because I waited or was a good friend. And I'm sorry for how I handled it today.

"I just think"—Imani starts, pulling back to look me in my eyes—"neither of us were seeing each other for who we are. And that's not fair."

She's right. Maybe neither of us have been seeing each other clearly for a long time, but I'm hoping this is the beginning of something new between us. Something better. She hasn't forgiven me yet, but I have hope that she will. That we can fix this. That this is a relationship worth fighting for.

"Hey." She looks down at my hands in my lap and runs her index finger across her ring. "You grabbed it."

When she raises her head, I take in her face: eyes soft, lips turned up just a little at the edges. I nod, but don't add anything. I want to give her the space to say everything she needs to right now.

"I saw what you posted on Confidential, by the way," she adds. She brushes a blade of grass from my shoulder. "You were really brave. I'm proud of you."

I don't know what's going to happen with the video, or with Troy. But now it's out there. At least I was honest. I read a Zora Neale Hurston quote once that said, "If you are silent about your pain, they'll kill you and say you enjoyed it."

Well, I refuse to be silent anymore. I refuse to let someone make me feel guilty for wanting to be treated with respect.

I didn't do it for Imani, obviously, but hearing her say that feels good. Great, even.

I hold out my pinky and go with the most sacred promise there is. "Friends forever?"

She looks at my hand between our faces for a second, and I'm worried she might not take my promise for what it is after how many I've managed to break lately. When she smiles and links her pinky with mine, it feels like I'm lit up from the inside out.

"Deal," she says. She kisses her thumb and I kiss mine, and I know that no matter what, this is a relationship I'm never going to stop working for.

"Ladies!" Peter jogs up and immediately cuts our heartfelt moment short as he stops to put his hands on his knees. He's out of breath like he ran all the way here from the Core. "I'm glad you're both here."

"You asked us to be, Peter," Imani responds, unimpressed as ever.

"Good point." He straightens up then and presses his lips together in a thin line. Peter is solemn as he paces in front of us. His usual backward Oakland A's cap is in his hands, and he twists it around nervously. This is such a far cry from his usual look that I'm a little scared by what he might say next.

"Imani, I owe you an apology," he says seriously. It's the first time I've seen that expression on his face all weekend, and it throws me just a bit.

Imani slaps her hand over her face and groans. "Peter, we. Weren't. Together. You don't owe me anything. You can kiss who-ever you want."

"No, no, that's not what I mean." He shakes his head. "And we didn't kiss! But. Okay, never mind. That's not the point. The point is, I snapped at you last night, and I shouldn't have. I wanted you to be into me like I was into you just because you were, like, nice to me, and then lashed out when you weren't. It was a dick thing to do."

For a second, her lips hang open and no words come out. I think she might need a system reboot.

"Imani?" I nudge her slightly.

"Yeah." She shakes her head. "Sorry, um. Thank you. For, um, saying that. I'm not used to . . . This is a lot of apologies today. So. Thank you. It's okay."

Peter beams and immediately throws his arms open for a hug. "Permission to approach the bench, you honor?"

Imani rolls her eyes but quirks up the corner of one of her lips. "Permission granted, you overgrown child."

Peter envelops her in a huge hug and lifts her off the ground. Imani's face goes a little red at all the affection, but she pats him on the back before he sets her back down on the ground.

"Now, look. I need both of you to come with me immediately. There is some very serious business that needs attending to, and your collective presence is required."

He pulls his hat on backward and does a two-finger point in our direction. Imani trudges after him, looking like someone is pulling her by the teeth. I laugh, and she shoots me a dirty look that quickly morphs into a smile of her own. It's not open arms, but it's something. I'll take it for now.

I realize that as much as I like Toni, as much as I wish things between us could work out, I don't *have* to be with her. I don't need to be on the receiving end of her attention to feel whole. Not anymore. From now on, I'm going to fight to be Olivia Brooks, in all her flawed glory, and have that be enough. I have a long way to go, and I have a lot of repairs to make, but right here is a good place to start.

≥TONI≤

SUNDAY NIGHT

I am big enough to admit that I would've used just about any excuse to text Olivia, but telling her we won the Golden Apple is a pretty good one. She doesn't respond for a full two hours, and when she does, my heart sinks. The message is so short and clinical, it reads like a goodbye.

> **It was always your show anyway.**
> **You'll be great. Good luck.**

I try not to think too much about it or let it dissuade me. It's a little succinct in a way Olivia rarely is, but that doesn't mean there's no hope of this plan working out. That doesn't mean everything that happened before my misguided breakup maneuver this morning triggered the worst possible course of events. Now all I can do is hope things go off as planned.

When Peter takes off to meet Olivia and Imani, I head to the main stage for a brief rehearsal and sound check. When I arrive backstage for rehearsal a few hours before the set, Teela is the first one to greet me.

"You must be Toni!" She smiles, and if I could melt into my boots right here, I would. I'm reminded that all the rumors are true: She's just as gorgeous in person as she is on TV. She's shaved her usual jet-black hair down to a buzz and dyed it blond and she's wearing a faux-leather go-go dress. Olivia would love it. "I'm looking forward to playing with you for real tonight."

I mumble a thank-you, but I'm interrupted by a tech guy who runs out a beautiful gold Epiphone Les Paul Standard. Teela smiles at him kindly, eyes crinkling at the corners, and explains that she needs the Epiphone Les Paul *Special* instead.

"We're down a guitar tech right now, so things are a little wonky," she explains when he rushes away, apologizing all the while. "And people keep believing this ridiculous rumor that I'm pregnant and we're going on hiatus, so finding a replacement has been a mess." She shakes her head and adjusts her in-ear. Her eye catches on my battered case on the ground next to me. I'm almost self-conscious about how worn and bruised it looks until she says, "I had a friend with a case just like that. He had this thing about remembering every show and every city. "

Her eyes go kind of soft and sad, and I make the connection for her.

"This was my dad's guitar case," I say. I try to keep my voice steady. "Jackson Foster."

Her mouth drops open, and I can see as she pieces the puzzle everything together.

"Toni . . . You're Jackson's Toni." She presses both hands against her cheeks and shakes her head. "Davey's gonna get a kick out of this."

My mom isn't going to believe the odds, that somehow both me and my dad ended up in this same incredible, impossible position nearly two decades apart, both on the precipice of the rest of our lives. It feels like a sign. My mom found what she loved, made a career of it, and never once left me to wonder how much I meant to her. Maybe I could be more than a collection plate full of my parents' anxieties. Maybe I could find a way to love wholly, and fiercely, without having to settle for one or the other.

"If you guys are looking for a guitar tech," I say as the kick drum sounds loud and brash on stage behind us. It feels like it matches the way my heart is beating. "I have some experience." I shrug. "It's practically in my blood."

She purses her lips, and waves over a woman nearby. She marches toward us with a headset on, face flushed and skin dewy from the humidity. Her hair is falling out of its low ponytail, and her all-black outfit is sweat-stained around her neck and under her arms. I know immediately that this is the woman who runs things around here.

"Toni, this is Meredith, our production manager." She gestures to me. "Mere, Toni is a whiz with guitars. Jackson's daughter. You think we have room for her on the European leg?"

The conversation is rushed, but clear. Meredith tells me to call her the next morning, and instructs me to find my passport.

"Teela," I say, after Meredith leaves to chase down their sound tech. Teela smiles encouragingly and I try to swallow down my nerves. This is a big ask, and definitely a risk, but I have to do it. "Would you mind if we didn't play a Kittredge song together tonight? There's something really . . . important to me I really want to try."

She puts her hands on her hips and shakes her head, but she never loses the smile.

"One of those Truths, huh?" she asks, repeating my dad's words like it's the most natural thing in the world. "You're a lot like your dad, you know."

And for once, the thought of being like my dad isn't terrifying. It feels like a compliment.

"I'd be honored," she adds.

There's so much still up in the air, more things left to figure out than I can count. But this moment is something. Taking this chance? Might just be everything.

Whatever plan I was looking for this weekend, I think I finally found it.

The rehearsal feels like it ends before I even realize what we've done, everything is so surreal. We play through the song a few times, another crew person walks me through my cues, and before I know it, it's time for the show to begin. The normally huge crowd at the last show of the weekend is a little smaller than usual, but still massive. I watch as people file in until the grass seems to be covered in Farmers for miles. When the show starts, the sheer volume of their shouts alone fills the entire place like there are closer to a million people than tens of thousands.

The stand-in guitar tech from earlier accidentally bumps into me on his way to run Davey's black-and-white left-handed Strat out to him on stage, and whispers an apology as he goes. The crew is busy making sure the show runs smoothly, the scale of the production bigger than anyone expected now that there are so many artists and bands to consider. I look to my left and see Bonnie Harrison leaning against a support beam and sipping a bottle of water and I think I might throw up a little. How often do you get to stand next to your idols? Perform on the same stage as them? The thought of it gives me such a head rush I wonder if anyone would notice me lying down just for a second as I collected myself.

In front of me, I watch Davey command the audience like he

was born to do it. His long red hair flies around his face as he speaks between songs. The set only started fifteen minutes ago, but it already feels like they've been out there for hours.

Kittredge was barely through their first song, "More Than Ruins," before two people in VIP were crowd-surfing to the metal barrier at the front of the stage. There are so many homemade signs and totems that you can barely see through to the back of the crowd. People with tapestries hastily painted with FARM-LAND IS FOREVER and THIS IS STILL OUR HOME on them wave their offerings high above their heads, a message they refuse to allow anyone to miss.

But it's the cacophony that never quite stops—while they sing, in between songs—that makes this different from any Farmland set I've ever been to. The constant roar of the mass of people in the audience shakes the ground and makes the hairs on my arm stand up. It's boisterous and unapologetic and unafraid. It's the most beautiful sound I've ever heard.

"You know"—Davey grips the mic with one hand and wraps the other around the neck of the guitar he's just pulled on—"there are a lot of people who don't think we should be here tonight." His voice booms out over the crowd, amplified even more than usual to overcome the sound of the rain now pouring down around us. "People who think that Farmland can be derailed by fear."

Everyone in the crowd erupts at that. The sound is thunderous, immovable. These people refuse to be scared into submission. I understand the Farmers who took off earlier this afternoon, who figured they should be better safe than sorry, but there's something about the audience in front of the stage that makes even the threat of nightmare worth this corner of the dream.

Sonny Blue is coming out to join them for a few songs later since their set the night before was canceled, and after that, the lead singer from Odd Ones is doing a cover of a Queen song with Davey, and then Pop Top is doing a brand-new single from her upcoming album, and even DJ Louddoc will be involved to put a house music spin on some of Kittredge's folksier songs. All of the biggest acts of the weekend are rallying together tonight in the spirit of Farmland.

"There are people who think we will be silent and scared," he continues, each line met with more cheers. "But those people don't know Farmland like I know Farmland. Those people don't understand the Farmer Code."

His voices cracks with emotion and it ripples through all of us like a flood. This Farmland may have scared us in a way none has before, but this place, what it means, can't be stolen from us.

"Out here, we look out for one another. This is a family."

This place has never been without its problems, but despite it all, it's always been a home to me. These people are *my* people. Farmland has always changed my priorities. On the grounds, I've been able to lower my defenses and allow myself to feel all the things I'm too afraid to feel otherwise.

It's that openness that made space for Olivia, and I'll never stop being grateful for it.

Davey explains that on the screens next to the stage there is a number that people can text to donate money to the Newtown Action Alliance, the charity founded in the wake of the Sandy Hook shooting. The entire time I was working on my song in the bus earlier, this is what the band was working out, and to see it set in motion is incredible.

I'm filled with a whole different set of nerves. I can still feel the sticky dampness that accompanies humidity and rain even after you've dried off, but I warm at the thought of what's to come. Even if Olivia doesn't want me back after this or doesn't want to give us a real shot, at least I'll have tried. I can live with the heartbreak if she doesn't want to give it one more go. Hell, maybe she won't be in the audience at all. But I have to do this.

For the first time in my life, I'm going to place my heart in someone else's hands and trust them to hold it with care. And if she's willing, I'm going to do the same in return.

"Miss Jackson?" One of the crew guys taps me on my shoulder and smiles. He holds up a pair of in-ears and gestures to my waistband before I give him a smile as a go-ahead.

He's a little jittery, his shaggy dishwater-blond hair disheveled as he reaches out to help me attach my wireless receiver to the back of my jeans, and I can tell he's new to the team. If my dad were here, I know he would've gone out of his way to make this kid feel seen.

When my in-ears are in and I've pulled the strap of my guitar securely over my head, careful not to dislodge my hat, I do some quick stretches. Nothing dramatic, since it's not like I'll be playing an entire show, jumping off the drummer's raised platform and doing standing backflips like Davey sometimes does, but enough to get my blood pumping.

"You're on next, Miss Jackson," the guy says, ducking in close so I can hear him over the calamity on stage. Teela is belting the chorus of one of their oldest songs, "If I Ever Leave This Place," a song about mortality and fate and fighting for what you believe in, and the band is gearing up for the breakdown. It's loud and chaotic and somehow perfectly contained. It's one of Kittredge's statement pieces. It hits different tonight.

I turn to the guy. "What's your name?"

"Deacon!" he shouts back. "This is my first time out with the band. I just came over from Megan Thee Stallion's tour. This is . . . different."

I laugh. I bet it is.

"I'm Toni." I hold my hand out and he shakes it quickly.

I pause for a second to think about how I want to introduce myself to him. Tonight, I'm on stage with the band, but that's not the role I expected to play. It's not even the role I'm sure I want past tonight.

I'm waiting in the wings for this band that I've grown up both resenting for taking my dad from me for so much of the year and admiring for being so undeniably, obnoxiously *good*. The truth is, I've been waiting in the wings for a long time.

In a week, I could be crewing for Kittredge halfway across the world, doing this, *feeling* this every night. Or I could be sitting in a classroom in Bloomington, going over syllabi for classes I don't care about and wondering why my roommate's socks make our dorm smell like expired pimento loaf. The question has never been *Where do I want to be?* so much as it is *What do I want my life to look like?*

I know now that I didn't need to perform on this stage to find the clarity my dad found here. In six months, a year, five years, what's going to matter to me is feeling as connected to another person, a mass of people, the way I have this weekend.

I remember my dad telling me once where they got the name Farmland Music and Arts Festival from. The whole lot used to be pure North Georgian farmland. To look at it now, the way it's covered entirely in metal stages and rental RVs and big neon lights, you wouldn't assume that it was at one point the south's leading purveyor of organic apple trees and GMO-free honey. You can become so good at being one thing, and then, by miracle or magic or capitalism, become something else entirely. Something no one would have expected.

Olivia was right: The answer was right there, at the tip of my fingertips, waiting for me all along. Wanting to pursue music in some way doesn't make me as inconsistent as my father any more than going to IU would make me stable like my mother. There is a middle ground, one that I didn't even think to explore, and that middle ground is me.

"I think I'll be with you guys for the next leg of the tour." His eyes widen in question. I add, "Backline."